DROP OF BLOOD

CITY OF BLOOD #1

LAURA GREENWOOD

© 2020 Laura Greenwood

All rights reserved. This book or parts thereof may not be reproduced in any form, stored in any retrieval system, or transmitted in any form by any means – electronic, mechanical, photocopy, recording or otherwise – without prior written permission of the published, except as provided by United States of America copyright law. For permission requests, write to the publisher at "Attention: Permissions Coordinator," at the email address; lauragreenwood@authorlauragreenwood.co.uk.

Visit Laura Greenwood's website at:

www.authorlauragreenwood.co.uk

Cover Design by Bella's Belles

Drop Of Blood is a work of fiction. Names, characters, places, and incidents are the products of the author's imagination or are used fictitiously. Any resemblance to actual persons, living or dead, businesses, companies, events, or locales is entirely coincidental.

BLURB

Blurb

The City Of Blood is dangerous, even for a vampire like me.

And yet, I'm here undercover, trying to find the smoking gun we need to bring it down. But staying out of trouble isn't as easy as following the rules. Anyone can be snatched up and forced into the cage fights. Or worse, be executed at dawn. All you have to do is breath wrong.

When I finally get a chance to join the resistance, I jump at the chance. Anything is better than the hell we're living.

One wrong step, and lives will be lost...including my own.

-

Drop Of Blood is book one of the City Of Blood series, a gritty vampire urban fantasy with a slow burn (m/f) romantic sub-plot.

CHAPTER ONE

I HATE RAIN. Especially this kind. It makes everything wet, but it's not heavy enough to dodge the drops, even with super speed. I sigh and push a strand of sodden hair behind my ear. I need to check-in at the town hall or I'm going to find myself in a sticky situation, rain or no rain.

Other vampires walk the streets along with me, none of us saying a word to one another. That's how it goes here. It's too dangerous to get close to anyone, and no one wants to risk their life for a stranger. The humans in this city think they have it bad, but they truly have no idea.

The worst thing is, I chose to come here. Vampires live in normal society in the rest of the country. We're represented on the government and have lives that don't involve having to check-in at the town hall every week just so they know we're still alive. I'm sure there's more to it, but I can't put my finger on what.

I run up the steps, taking two at a time with ease. I suppose that's one advantage of living in this place, the blood supply is more than steady. It's plentiful. Though that raises a whole slew of questions about where the blood comes from in the first place. I try my best to consume the ethically sourced stuff, but without taking it straight from the vein, then there's no way to be completely sure. And even then, there are doubts. Forcing people to donate blood isn't unusual here. And I'm sure the bounty of blood can be taken away as easily as it's given. One day, it will be.

I join the line of vampires waiting for their check-in. Some check their phones, others just twiddle their thumbs or strike up random conversations. It's both normal and surreal. Some of the people around me will have been in the city for the entire thirty years it's been a thing. Others will have arrived later, having believed the rubbish spouted about this being a vampire's paradise. Everything they say is a lie. Something I knew even before I came here.

My mind strays to the same question it does every time I have to check-in. Was it a mistake for me to agree to come here? Most of the time, I'm sure I'm doing the right thing. But now it's raining, I'm not so sure.

I shouldn't think like this. It's dangerous. No one is my friend here. I can't let them be.

I shake my head. No one here can read minds, it's not a trick vampires are capable of. But that doesn't mean that no one can read the direction of my thoughts from the expression on my face. And in this city, the wrong face is enough to get someone arrested, never to be seen again. I'm not ready to die. Which means toeing the line like a good little vampire.

"Next," the bored woman behind the desk calls.

The line moves forward. I don't understand why it always takes so long to do this. They must do the same thing for everyone, and the same thing day in, day out. Everyone is given a day they have to come, and very few people miss it.

"Next."

The line moves again.

There's only one more person and then it's my turn. As normal, the butterflies in my stomach kick into overdrive. I should be used to this by now, but instead, I think it only gets worse. And yet, there's no reason for it to. I'm here legally. We thought that bit of the plan through.

"Next."

"Hi." I flash her the best smile I can, making sure I show off some fang as I do so. She's supposed to check I have them. Which is ridiculous considering we're already proven vampires.

"ID?" Up close, she looks even more board. I hadn't thought it would be possible.

I slide it across to her. She picks it up and scans it through the machine.

It beeps to let us know I've been processed, and then she hands it back to me. "Done."

"Thank you." I smile again, but for no reason. She's already moved on to the next person. This must be the hundredth check she's done for me, but I still don't know her name. It's the same for other people. The less contact there is, the fewer chances there are that someone you care about will be carted off and killed. It's that kind of world.

I turn away from the rest of the vampires and head back out onto the street. The rain has gotten heavier while I did my thing. Great. All I need. I'm going to arrive at work sopping wet and without a change of clothes. Normally, I'd bring one with me, but it's best not to do anything like that on check-in day.

Water splashes from the pavement onto my boots. Everyone around me is doing the same, with very few people opting to use anything else. No one bothers with cars because there's nowhere to go in them. If someone drives past, they're likely to be an official and it's best to dive for cover. And as for the buses...they're far too expensive for what they are. Which leaves walking.

"Hi Bernice," I say as I push through the door and into the office.

"Hey, Chloe. Check-in today?" she says, eyeing the state of my outfit.

"Yep."

"You should start keeping a spare set of clothes here. That's what I do."

I grimace. It's not a bad idea overall, but it *is* a bad idea for me. It's best I don't leave traces of myself everywhere. Not that I can explain that to her.

Sometimes, having a double life is tiring. Even more so when I remember it means no friends, no boyfriends, and no place to call home. I don't count my tiny apartment in the city. I didn't choose it, and there's nothing there that truly shows me. The first week here, I tried not to sleep at all in case I left too much DNA everywhere, but I realised that was impossible soon enough. Now, I opt for trying to *only* leave traces of me at my apartment.

I drop myself into my desk chair, ignoring the squelch of fabric as I do. I kick off my boots and wiggle my toes, enjoying at least one part of my body being dry.

"Did you hear about the event this weekend?" Bernice asks over her computer screen.

My machine is still starting up. The technology here has moved on enough since the founding to get by, but not as much as it has in the outside world. As soon as I'd got here, I'd had to buy myself a new phone in case anyone noticed my old one was too fancy. I could have explained it as being because I was new to the city, but it's best not to draw attention to anything that makes you stand out.

"Huh, no? What happened?" I act as if I'm not interested despite the fact I am. This is the kind of thing I should report back when I'm called upon again.

"I don't know, but there's an email gone out. I'll forward it to you." She clicks on a couple of buttons.

I want to tell her no, but it's too late. "Do you have the link where I can sign up for stuff like this?" I ask, even though it's out of character. I'm supposed to act as if I don't care about what goes on in the city, but this is too important.

"Sure. But I thought you didn't follow this stuff?"

Damn. I've gone and acted suspicious.

I shrug. "I just want to know when I shouldn't plan anything. You know how it gets when there's some kind of fight on." At least, I'm guessing it's one of the cage fights. Despite it being near the top of my list of things I need to find out about, I haven't been able to get to one since I got here. And now I'm finding out why. Apparently, corporal punishment isn't something open to the public.

"Ah, good point." She hits a button. "Sent it to you."

"Thanks, Bernice." I turn my attention back to my screen, which has finally come to life, and pull up my emails. There's a couple from clients, but nothing urgent. Instead, I focus on the two Bernice sent me.

The one with the sign-up link, I forward to an innocuous email address that would bounce around five different servers before hitting the person it needs to. Hopefully, they can then sign up for the alerts and get the intel straight to their inboxes. It'll save some heavily coded messages on both sides that way.

After signing up with my own email address lest Bernice get suspicious, I turn to her other email.

The sick feeling starts in the pit of my stomach. *Fights.* Lots of them. Which is just a slightly less obvious way of saying executions. Sometimes, I wish they'd simply outright say what they mean, but I understand that's not how it works. I scan the list of names, unsure what I'm looking for. It's not likely I'll recognise any of them. I don't know enough people here. I wonder what they all did to deserve this.

Probably nothing.

"Are you going to go?" Bernice asks.

I jump, not realising she's looking over my shoulder.

I shake my head. "It's not my thing." Despite that, I will be there, but under one of aliases. While my ID isn't a lie, it's not the only name I'm known by in the city. It isn't possible to find out everything I need to while using my real name.

But Bernice doesn't need to know that. As far as she knows, I'm nothing more than her fellow marketing assistant. I do my work and live an ordinary life.

She'll never know how wrong she is.

CHAPTER TWO

THE DOOR SLAMS shut behind me, and I relax for the first time all day. This place may not be home, but it's the closest I've got while I'm living here, and it's my safe haven for that reason. I don't share where it is with anyone other than the people I have to. If I could keep it away from the authorities, I would do too, but that would raise too many suspicions.

"Hello?" I call out.

No one answers. That's good. The first thing I want to do now is strip out of the wet clothes and get a shower. Which I can't do if someone wants to talk to me about what I've found out. I'm glad no one's here for another reason, though. I have nothing to tell them. Sometimes, I think I'm the worst spy ever.

I strip off my clothes and dump them in a pile on

the floor of my bedroom. At least this place came with an en-suite. It's not something I have back at my normal vampire den, and I enjoy the privacy, even if it comes at the cost of my entire social life.

As soon as I'm in the shower, the stress of my day melts away. Something about the soggy remnants of this morning's rain put me in a foul mood for the rest of it, only made worse by clients who didn't seem to understand what they want from their marketing campaigns. Or that I'm nothing more than a low-level worker. I can't answer questions about how much each thing will cost them, and why everything is behind schedule.

I close my eyes and let the hot water run down my face. At least the City Of Blood doesn't torture its residents with bad water pressure. That would make things ten times harder to deal with.

I prolong my shower for as long as I can, knowing that when I get out, I have to deal with what I learned today. Including the long list of people who are heading towards the cage fights. I doubt any of them deserve what's coming their way. But there's no one to save them.

I thought I understood the phrase *every man for himself* before, but I was wrong. It's only since coming here that I've discovered the true meaning. Even in the short months I've been here, I've seen people turned over to the authorities by their own families, or by their best friend. People die in the streets at least once a week, and that's without the executions I've heard about.

But what gets to the outside world is carefully controlled. I heard about a lot of the things I'm seeing here but didn't understand the extent of them. If the outside world finds out what goes on here, then they'll be able to put a stop to it.

Which is why I'm here. To watch, learn, and report back. If I do my job, they'll be able to shut down the City Of Blood once and for all. If I fail, then I'll be dead, and none of it will matter to me.

I shut off the water and get out, wrapping myself in one of the thick towels I splurged on. At least the danger pay is a perk of being a spy and risking certain death.

My stomach rumbles, reminding me it's time to eat and drink. I like to take my blood with food, it feels a lot more civilised, though I know a lot of vampires don't feel that way.

I pad to the kitchen and pull a blood bag out of the cupboard. They may not last as long as keeping them in the fridge, but I prefer my blood room temperature, and I have to leave my apartment every day anyway, so it's not like I have to go out of my way to buy rations every couple of days. I pour it into a mug and drink some of it down, feeling instantly refreshed. It's amazing what ills a good mug of blood will chase away.

A siren blares through the apartment, making me jump. I'm not sure why, I should know what time dawn is. I grab my *good* phone from where I left it earlier and use the app on it to close the blinds. I may not use this one outside of my apartment, but it has it's uses while inside it. Most vampires will be running around pulling their curtains and blinds closed right now, while I can avoid turning into a crisp with nothing more than the touch of a button.

Which gives me a chance to check the notification flashing at the top of the screen.

A mission.

Kind of. Calling it a mission is probably going too far. In reality, it'll just be a message from one of my handlers outside the walls telling me I'm doing a good job, or something like that. I think it's supposed to keep my morale up. It doesn't work. I doubt anything could.

I click on it without paying much attention. My focus is on what I can eat for dinner. I need to go shopping but haven't had the time yet. A toasted bagel with cream cheese it is.

I'm halfway through putting my bagel in the

toaster when I realise I haven't checked the message, just opened it.

With a sigh, I unlock my phone again and stare at the word on the screen.

Go.

It takes a moment for the meaning to sink in. They want me to go to the cage fights. I thought they might and was already preparing to. But it's now an official instruction. It's amazing how much can be conveyed in one word. But we have to use a heavy code if we want to send more than that or do what I did earlier and send through a chain of emails. But the latter is only for me sending information out. It's too dangerous for incoming emails. Not when we don't know anything about what kind of detective systems they have in place.

The bagel pops out of the toaster, but my stomach is too twisted up in knots to eat it right now. I'll come back to it later.

First, I have to work out my plan for the cage fights. I was going to use one of my false identities to go, but perhaps that isn't the best idea. Not if I need to go back several times.

For my first trip into hell, I'll just be plain old Chloe Simons. If I do my job right, no one will remember me anyway.

CHAPTER THREE

VAMPIRES ARE EVERYWHERE. I'm not sure what I expected when I set off from my apartment, but this isn't it. Everyone is chatting away, and buying food from vendors, and even placing bets on who will do well, and who will die.

It's a constant fight to keep my face neutral. I can't draw attention to myself by letting my feelings show on my face. That's a good way to get myself thrown into one of these fights myself. That'll do no one any good, least of all me.

Despite the urge to stand at the side and not pay attention to anything going on around me, I know that isn't an option. I need to talk to people and find out more about what's going on. If I'm lucky, I might find someone else who is new here, and tag along with them. Though excitement seems to be the biggest thing here.

"New here?" a gruff voice asks.

I turn to find a bulky vampire standing behind me with his arms crossed, a gesture which only accentuates his bulging muscles.

I gulp away my fear, not wanting him to see it. "That obvious?"

He chuckles. "I had the same look on my face when I started to work here. It wears off."

I nod, at a loss for what to say. I've never thought about the fact people work here. But of course they do. Who else will deal with the prisoners, guests, and clean up?

"If you're hungry, there's carts all around. You'll find blood, coffee, and a lot of fried snacks," he says, pointing to several of them as he speaks. "Avoid the burger place at the end. Their meat is nasty." He shudders.

I pull up a weak smile, hoping he puts it down to nerves. "Thanks."

"You probably just want to watch, if it's your first time. But if you want to place bets, you're better off on the main floor than up here. Plus, you can be closer to the action," he continues.

"How will I know who to bet on?" The knot in my stomach twists again as I realise I'm probably going to have to go through with a bet so I know how it works. I'm starting to regret agreeing to this job. I'm not sure why I thought I could do it when it needs an agent with far more experience than I have.

"See that girl over there with the programs?" He points to her.

"Yes."

"Go get one from her. Say Vinnie sent you and she'll give you one of the beginner ones. You want new people who are still healthy and strong, or those on their tenth fight," he tells me.

My eyebrows knit together. "Why people on their tenth fight?" The new people, I understand. I doubt they do a lot to look after the people they have trapped here. But surely that means people who are going into their tenth fight will be at a severe disadvantage.

He glances around, as if to check who else is close to us, then leans in. "Because they're told that if they win their tenth fight, then they get set free."

My eyes widen. "Is it true?" The question is out of my mouth before I can think to stop it. Hopefully, Vinnie takes it to mean I don't want dangerous people out on the streets again.

He shakes his head. "I've never seen anyone walk away from here. I don't know what happens to the people who win their tenth fight. Those that get there often do. But they aren't let go."

I bite my lip and nod. It makes sense. The point of sending people here is to get rid of them.

"Why are you telling me all of this?" I ask him. Couldn't he get into trouble for it? Or is he testing me?

He shrugs. "Sometimes people look a little lost. I have to live with myself at the end of each day and helping them is one of the ways I do it."

"Oh."

Before I can say anything else, he disappears into the crowd again. I'm not sure if I just got marked as someone to watch, or if he's genuinely trying to help. I'll have to wait and see on that front.

I steel my nerves and head over to the girl he pointed out. She's giving out programs left, right, and centre, as people make their way into the main fighting area. The whole thing feels more like we're about to go in to see a highly anticipated play, rather than seeing people fight to the death.

Someone bumps into my shoulder, and instantly, I'm on alert.

I turn to face him, finding a handsome man, not much older than I am, standing there.

"Sorry," he mumbles, then heads on his way again, not waiting for my reply.

But I'm transfixed. What's a human doing here? There's plenty of people around, but none of them are human. No, wait, one of them is. And he just bumped into me. My fangs descend, the scent of his blood having taken me off guard. I can control my urges, but sometimes it's hard not to let natural instincts take over. And this is one of those cases.

I tear my gaze away from his retreating back, knowing I need to focus on my mission and not on the mystery man. Without talking to him, I have no way of knowing if he has reasons. It's best to focus on what I'm here for and nothing else.

"Vinnie sent me," I say to the girl when it's my turn.

She smiles and reaches into her bag, pulling out a slightly different program. "Five pounds, please," she says.

I hand over the money and gingerly take the program from her. I'm not sure how I feel about what's inside, and it's making it hard to act naturally.

"Thank you," I mutter.

A lone seat in the corner catches my eye, so I make my way over to it. The hard stone isn't very comfortable, but I'm not going to be here for long. I just want to flick through the program before I go onto the main floor. I don't want any surprises once I am.

The nausea intensifies as I scan the pages. They're treating people like horses at a race. There are all the stats I could want about each of them, including whether they're vampire or human. It seems like there's a mix of both, but vampires seem to be most common. Especially among those who are beyond their first fight.

Tears prick the corners of my eyes, but I force them away. I must stay strong. If I look as if I'm faltering, then it'll be me next. And if they work out that I'm spying for Dimitri and the vampires outside the city, they'll probably torture me for what I know. Which isn't much. Thankfully. But it'll hurt, and I'd rather not deal with the pain, if I don't have to.

A bell rings out, signalling that the first fight will begin in a couple of minutes. I memorise the names of the three humans and two vampires involved, knowing no one else will bother. They're here for the bloodshed. To them, it's nothing more than sport.

I rise to my feet and follow the crowds inside, trying to stay towards the middle so I don't draw too much attention from anyone. I don't want to seem too eager, or too reluctant. There's a balance to strike in being forgettable.

I brush a strand of dark brown hair behind my ear, wishing I'd thought to wear it up. Not that it'll make a difference. Besides, having it loose means I can hide my face a little and be harder to recognise.

"Last call for bets!" one of the bookies calls.

Someone pushes me to the side to get to him. I rub my shoulder, but don't make a big deal out of it.

I must be forgettable.

I'd like to think I'm not the hot-headed vamp type, but people can push me too far, and I worry that's going to happen here.

"The fight is about to begin. All betting is now to cease," an automated voice comes over the speakers.

The whole room falls still as a ding sounds, and it isn't hard to work out why. The fight's participants are shoved out into the huge cage at the centre of the room. A woman of around forty breaks from the others and rushes to the bars and tries to sneak through them.

A guard steps forward and prods her with a stick.

Her yelp of pain turns my stomach. I'm glad I didn't eat before I came here.

Two more people are shoved into the cage next. My heart sinks. I've been lucky enough never to have starved for blood in my life, but the same can't be said of the two vampires in front of me. The taller of the two shrinks back against the corner of the cage, trying to get as far away from the humans as possible. No doubt he realises that the moment one of them gets a cut, his instincts will take over and he'll drain them dry.

The woman with him isn't as cautious. It's hard to tell from this far away, but I think she's further gone into starvation than he is. It's a cruel tactic, and one that will mean the humans stand next to no chance.

Another of the guards steps up and pokes one of the humans, causing another shout of pain and the scent of blood to fill the stadium.

Bile rises in my throat, and it's hard to breathe, even though I know I have to.

I'm here to put a stop to this. I repeat the words in my head, but they're barely helping. I can't believe I've become a part of this. I've spent money coming here and ploughed it back into the city. Am I guilty of keeping it going?

The female vampire wastes no time scenting the blood. She crouches down, preparing to launch herself at the group of humans. As much as I want to look away from what's happening, I can't. Something about it is mesmerising. Though perhaps that's the wrong word. It almost makes it seem like I'm enjoying myself when I'm definitely not.

Before she has a chance to pounce, the male vampire darts forward and takes her head in his hands.

My heartbeat races, adrenaline filling me as if *I'm* the one about to die.

With one swift move, he snaps her neck. It wouldn't be possible for a human to do that, but he has the advantage of having more strength, even if he is short on blood.

Cheers sound from across the room, with the occasional groan or annoyed grumble, presumably from people who were betting on the woman to win.

The female vampire's body slumps to the ground, and the attacker retreats to his corner, closing his eyes and moving his lips in what I can only assume is a distraction technique. Even I can smell the blood, and I'm not starving, or as close to it. The scent must be driving him crazy.

"Mum!" someone shouts from the crowd.

I search around for the owner of the voice to find a petite woman pushing through the people.

"Mum, please. Mum, no. Get up. Please..." Her begging turns to sobs as the reality sets in.

I can't take it any longer. I know I'll probably have to come back here, but hopefully it will be after I've had some time to prepare. This is barbaric. No, worse than that. It's cruel, and unnecessary, and I can't take a single moment more of it tonight.

Without even waiting for the fight to end, I turn on my heels and make my way out of the room. I need to go home and write my report, that way, the true horror of what I've witnessed will come through it.

The moment I step outside the building, I finally feel like I can breathe again. I close my eyes and count to ten, trying to maintain my composure. If anyone asks me what I'm doing, I'll have to make something up about bad blood, or they'll know I can't handle what's going on inside.

And that's a good way to gain myself a front-row seat.

I don't think I'd last a minute.

CHAPTER FOUR

I SLAM the door shut behind me, then double and triple check the locks the same way I have been every night since the cage fights. I'm not sure what I expected from them, but I didn't think they'd hit me this hard. No matter what I do, I can't get the images out of my mind. Instead of increasing my resolve to do my job and find a way to bring the City Of Blood down, it's only distracting me.

With the new latch I bought firmly in place, I turn back to my small apartment. Loneliness creeps over me. There's no one who will cry out for me if I die.

"Hello?" I call out, the same as I do every time I come home.

"In the kitchen," a familiar voice answers.

Great. Just what I need. The one day I really

hoped there wouldn't be anyone waiting, there is. Probably on the back of what I wrote in my report.

I drop my bag by the door and make my way to where he's waiting.

Bram leans against my kitchen side, looking as if he didn't have a care in the world, and not like he's an illegal unregistered vampire in a city which kills people for less. I'd be too nervous in his shoes. But then again, he does his job the same way I do mine. With our eyes fully open to the consequences.

"How are things going?" he asks.

"Bad." I shrug. There's no point lying. The only reason we have check-ins like this is to make sure I'm handling my assignment well. It makes me a little uncomfortable thinking of him sneaking into the city for me. I'm not sure how he gets in. Which is the way things should be. The less I know, the less can be tortured out of me if I'm caught.

He nods knowingly. "As we suspected from your last message."

I sigh. "I don't understand why you can't just send in your girlfriend and her hunters," I mutter. The ex-vampire hunters would be done within days, and no one would have to get their hands dirty. Except them, of course. But they're used to it.

"Wife," he corrects instantly. "And because we

promised we wouldn't make them do that anymore." His expression hardens into one I'm not able to read.

From what I can tell, that's just part of his personality. Whatever happened to him when he was younger, he's as hard as nails now, and not the kind of vampire anyone would want to mess with. Unless he's talking to his wife, that is.

I sigh dramatically. "I know, it's just wishful thinking."

He chuckles. "I'm sure there are others wondering the same thing," he admits. "But I'm not here to talk about alternative ways to end the city."

"Oh?" I raise an eyebrow. "Do you want me to go back to the cages?" The words almost stick in my throat, but I force them out. It's my job. I must remember that, no matter how disgusted I become. It's not like I've been sent to the city to get blueprints so they can build another one.

"Not yet," Bram answers, finally unfolding his arms from across his chest.

I resist the urge to tap my foot as my impatience grows. The longer he's here, the more in danger we both are.

"We need you to go to a party."

Is he serious? A party?

"Inside the city?" It doesn't make any sense to me.

How can they send me to a party after what I've seen?

"Yes." He picks a slim piece of card up from the kitchen side and hands it to me. I hadn't even noticed it sitting there.

I take it from him and scan the elegantly written words on it.

"You want me to go to one of the *Mayor's* parties?" It's impossible to keep the disbelief from my voice. I'm starting to realise why none of their other spies are still alive. This is reckless, to say the least.

"We need as much information as we can get."

"It seems risky," I mutter.

"It is," he admits. "We've never gotten anyone inside one of the Mayor's parties before."

That's because they keep sending vampires who look as if they've spent the past hundred years working out and drinking protein shakes. The unremarkable young woman approach is a new one.

Either that, or they couldn't find anyone more reckless than me to take the post.

"You'll be needing this," he adds.

I take the object from him, loving the feel of the smooth wood against my skin. When one of my fingers runs over a catch, I press it, and the wood splits in two, revealing a circular black fan. I click the two handles together. I turn it over to see if there's a pattern on the other side, only to be disappointed.

It's pretty, if a little boring.

"Why do I need this?" I ask, flipping it over a couple of times to see if there's something I've missed.

Bram shrugs. "I'm just the messenger. You're to take it to the party."

I want to make a snide comment about how useless his information is, but I bite my tongue. He's right. He's just the person telling me about my next job. It's not his fault we can't share many details.

"Fine." I glance at the invitation. Only two nights until I find out my answer. That'll have to be good enough.

"Oh, and one more thing," he says.

I raise an eyebrow and wait for him to continue.

"You'll need an appropriate dress for the party."

"Is nothing you supplied me with good enough?" Most of my clothes were here before I was. Now I think about it, I doubt any of them are suitable for the kind of event the Mayor holds.

"No."

I run through my finances in my head, trying not to panic about how much a suitable dress will cost.

"There's extra money in your account to cover the cost," he assures me quickly.

Relief floods through me. That's one less thing to worry about. "Thank you."

"Stay safe," he tells me, then heads towards the door. He'll be gone within minutes and we'll have gotten away with another meeting.

The moment I hear the door shut behind him, I rush to it and bolt all the locks again. They aren't likely to stop anyone who wants to get in to arrest me, but I still find reassurance in having them. And I have to make myself feel safe while here, or I'm never going to get my job done.

I lean against the wall, preparing myself mentally for the idea of dress shopping. I hate it on a normal day, but with so much at stake, I find I like the idea even less.

CHAPTER FIVE

Lights twinkle from each side of the path leading up to the Mayor's mansion. Everywhere I look, there are vampires making their way towards it, all dressed in their best. Luckily, the dress I've picked out seems to blend in with the rest of women. I'm glad I used the amount of money Bram and the others dropped into my account as the benchmark for how much I should be spending on a dress. At least I won't stand out.

The silk slides against my skin, reminding me I can't walk too fast for fear of ripping it. I hope I won't have to do any kind of running in it. If someone wants to arrest me, then I won't stand a chance of getting away.

Music drifts from the open doors, transporting me into another world. It's like something out of another time. I pause for a moment and open my clutch to check I have everything. There isn't much I can do if I haven't, it'll take me too long to get home and back. My city-safe phone nestles next to the odd fan Bram gave me. I still have no idea what I'm supposed to do with it, but it's better to have it with me. I pull out my invitation, unsure if I need it. I doubt anyone uninvited would try and turn up here, it's too dangerous.

With as much confidence as I can muster, I stride towards the entrance, determined to not draw attention to myself. I pass through the entrance without any problems. There isn't anyone even bothering to check invitations. I fumble with my clutch and shove the piece of card back in. Carrying it around when no one is looking for it will be a quick way to signal I'm up to no good.

I follow the other vampires through the corridor while hoping they're leading me in the right direction. The music is getting louder, which gives me hope.

Another set of double doors opens in front of us. My heels click on the floor, not making as much noise as some of the others as I opted to wear flat ones. My dress may not make it easy to run, but that doesn't mean my shoes should make it even more dangerous.

Voices chatter away over the music, rather ruining the beauty of the melody, but it does reassure me that I'm heading in the right direction after all.

I step into the room and stop in my tracks, trying to process what I'm seeing. It isn't until someone walks into me that I stumble forward and out of the way.

"Sorry," I mutter under my breath and hurry to the side. I've already spotted a refreshment table to the left, and plan to get myself a glass of something so I can look busy for at least a moment.

I make my way over while keeping an eye on the front centre of the room where a huge throne dominates. It's too much for me, but my opinion isn't going to change what the dark-haired vampire lounging in the chair thinks about her seating.

My drinking options are limited to blood and wine, so I opt for the latter. Something tells me it's the safest option. I pour myself a small glass of white wine. Once I have it, I place myself in a better position to observe the ballroom. Later, I'll attempt to listen in on some conversations, though I'm not sure what I'll learn. Hopefully, if they can get me invited to one of these events, then they'll be able to get me a second invitation. Maybe then I'll be able to get some useful information.

The wine is ice cold, as it should be, and the tartness of it is oddly refreshing. I study the Mayor over the rim of my glass, trying to get a measure of her. She appears younger than I expect, probably because she has the advantage of a vampire's lack of ageing. I'm not sure how old she is, but she's been running this city for nearly thirty years, which must make her sixty at the youngest. Not many vampires manage to climb to positions with this much power at that age anymore, so she's likely much older. It's still a mystery to me how she managed to set up the city in the first place. It's hard to think about it not being part of the world when it's been around three years longer than I have.

A woman in an ornate dress walks in front of my view and snaps a fan open. It's like the one I have, except that it's a warm yellow. A quick scan of the room reveals at least a dozen others with fans out, in all kinds of colours. It doesn't take long for me to spot several using black ones. I'm not sure if it means anything, as not all the women have them, but I do. Should I be using it?

I take another sip of wine to squash my nerves. I need to be careful I don't overdo it.

Thankfully, no one seems to be paying much attention to me, so I set my glass down and start making a lap of the room. The party is both everything I thought it would be, and nothing like it. So far, there's been no death, which is a good thing. But it also seems rather tame.

I'm making my second uninteresting lap around the room when the Mayor rises to her feet and claps her hands.

Silence falls instantly. Whether she does good things with it or not, there's no doubt she wields a lot of power, and knows how to use it. It's eerie how quiet the room is despite there being close to a hundred people in it. The soft rustle of fabric rubbing together, and the odd creak from the direction of the musicians, are the only sounds to reach my sensitive ears.

"Good night, my fellow children of blood," she starts, her voice ringing out through the room.

Everyone stares at her as if she's the messiah of vampire-kind. Personally, I don't see it. No one who uses the term *children of blood* to describe us is worth taking seriously. Normally, they're too self-involved to say anything of interest.

Uh-oh. That kind of thinking is going to get me killed if I'm not careful. Whether I like it or not, this woman is more in control of my life than I am. And as I'm here under my real name again, she'll make short work of figuring out my identity. It almost seems laughable that I have the multitude of

IDs I do, as there never seems to be a chance to use them.

"With the month of our anniversary upon us, I give you a gift," the Mayor announces, then claps her hands again.

Behind her, two hidden doors swing open, and a guard marches out of each of them. I focus my attention on the one on the left. I imagine they'll both be doing the same anyway, but even if they aren't, it's better that I give an accurate report on one side, than none.

The vampire tugs on something which clanks loudly. My blood turns to ice in my veins. Even if I can't see exactly what's coming, I have a good idea.

So much for thinking there isn't going to be any death tonight.

"The blood of the most beautiful humans in the city," the Mayor says, her mouth curving up into a satisfied smile as she watches. "Drink your fills and worry about nothing. They are yours."

Cheers come from some of the assembled vampires. I'm relieved it isn't all of them. It's reassuring to know not everyone in this city is unnecessarily cruel and hateful when it comes to their attitude towards humans.

The guard reaches a divot in the floor and attaches the chain to it. Five humans spread out around it, each at the end of another chain, and each wincing in pain. I don't know how the other vampires are managing to circle around them with lust in their gazes when I can hear their whimpers.

"Feast!" the Mayor shouts, then gestures for the musicians to begin playing again.

They choose a lively tune, one that doesn't fit the solemnness of the situation. Are the assembled vampires really okay with this? How can they let someone like this rule over them when she has no compassion for any kind of life?

"You have to smile," someone whispers beside me.

I jump, then turn. The only person there is a girl with a fan who is retreating quickly towards an alcove.

The fan...

I open my clutch and pull it out, clicking it open and into position so I can use it to hide my face. I'm not sure I can control my expression while this is happening. Covering it up seems like the best option.

The sweet tang of blood fills the air. My reflexes kick in as my fangs descend and hunger rumbles inside me. But the sensation quickly turns to disgust as I watch. I cover my face with the fan, noticing a few of the other girls do it too. I wave it a couple of times.

The wave of air against my skin is all I need to calm myself down. My fangs retract and the smell becomes nothing more than something I'm dimly aware of. I drank before I came, anticipating *something* putting me off doing it otherwise. Though I couldn't have imagined this.

"If you don't want a bite of the human, why don't you take one of me?" a man asks someone.

Poor girl.

A hand clamps around my wrist and I whimper in pain. The man pulls me around.

"Don't ignore me," he growls. "How much for the night?"

My eyes widen. What is he asking?

"I..."

"Lord Rufus, a moment, if you please." A woman swoops in and places a hand on his arm. A closed fan dangles from her wrist.

The man's fingers let up and I resist the urge to rub my wrist where it hurts. I'm going to have bruises in the morning.

"Lady Catherine," he acknowledges gruffly. "Your girl is ignoring me."

"Ah, I'm sorry about that. She's new and not taking clients tonight," she lies smoothly. At least, I hope she is, and she doesn't think I'm someone else.

He narrows his eyes at me. "She had her fan open."

Catherine nods. "Simply practice, My Lord. Tamsin will take care of you. On the house, of course." She gestures across the room for a pretty girl with bouncy blonde curls.

She heads our way instantly.

I look between all three parties, confused by what's going on, but no one seems to want to explain it to me.

"Very well," Lord Rufus grumbles, then turns his attention to the girl heading towards us, leaving me alone with my saviour.

"Thank you," I whisper, my voice cracking slightly. "I don't know what happened."

Catherine raises an eyebrow, as if not believing a word I'm saying. "What's your name?" she asks.

"Chloe."

"I'm Catherine," she says needlessly. "Why don't you come with me and we'll have a little chat."

The way she says it leaves no doubt in my mind that saying no isn't an option. I swallow down my nerves and follow her to a side room, hoping this isn't going to end badly. She saved me from the man, but that doesn't mean anything. Not here.

For all I know, she wants to get me alone so she can kill me herself.

CHAPTER SIX

A LOUD GULP escapes me the moment Catherine closes the door, leaving the two of us alone in the small room she's brought us to. I have no idea what's going on, but the sounds of the party are too far away for me to be completely comfortable. If she wants to kill me, then she'll have an easy job of it.

"Would you like some blood?" she asks, pulling out a hip flask and two shot glasses from her bag. It's bigger than my clutch, but for some reason, I'm still surprised that she has those things in there.

"I'm okay, thank you." My voice trembles as I speak.

Pull it together, Chloe. The words spin around my mind, but they don't help me gain control.

Catherine chuckles. "It's not the same stuff that's

in the other room, don't worry. You never want to drink that."

"Why not?" I ask.

She shrugs. "You saw what's going on in there."

She doesn't need to say anything else, I know what she means. I can't imagine the blood being served is any more ethically sourced than the humans currently chained to the floor.

I wonder if any of them are dead yet?

Bile rises in my throat. How can people come to a fancy event like this and kill someone? Or is that the reason *why* they come? I try not to think about that too much.

"Where did you get that fan?" Catherine asks, suddenly growing a lot more serious.

From the expression on her face, I doubt she's going to accept me finding it somewhere or any other lie.

"I was given it." There's no harm in admitting that, I don't think so, but who knows. I'm in over my head, even if I don't want to admit it.

"Interesting. By who?" Nothing about her feels like a threat, but I know that doesn't mean anything. She's probably powerful enough to snap my neck without a second thought.

I don't answer, hoping my silence buys me time to think about a way that doesn't reveal who I am.

"May I look at it?" she asks.

"Why?" I blurt.

She flashes me a wry smile. "Call it professional curiosity."

"In a fan?" Despite my reluctance, I hand it over. It's nothing more than paper and wood, it can't tell her anything.

She takes it from me and turns it over in her hands, studying every part of it.

"As I suspected."

She hands it back to me. I take it gingerly, wondering what she's thinking.

"What did you suspect?" I blurt, not being able to take not knowing. I really need to work on being more covert in how I bring things up and try to get information out of people. If I carry on this way, then I'm going to get caught sooner rather than later.

"The identity of the man who gave you that." She nods at the fan. "Or at least, the one who ordered it to be given to you."

I waver for a moment, considering telling her everything there and then, but I know I shouldn't. This may be some kind of test, either from my employers, or from the Mayor and her people. I'm not sure what will happen if I fail the former's test, but the latter consequence is easy to discern.

"It's best we don't discuss that any further," she says before I get a chance to speak.

I'm glad she's made the decision. It's easier for me that way.

"How do you know it isn't just a black fan?" I ask, revealing that it *isn't* just a fan. Though now I think about it, no one ever told me the fan is special or anything.

Catherine chuckles. "I'm the only person in the city who has these."

It's my turn to laugh. "I doubt you have the monopoly on fashion accessories."

Though I must admit she does *look* as if she could. Her dress is fancy in a way that makes her seem as if she's from another time. One long ago where all the women wore tailored dresses and fashion was about the size and shape of a skirt. Sometimes, I find myself wishing I lived in that time. It sounds fun. But I imagine it had its drawbacks too.

"This one, I do." She picks up her own fan and opens it, moving it with expert grace. Something I don't have.

"I'm not sure I understand," I mumble, hating that it's one more mystery to add to the rest.

"They didn't tell you what it is, did they?" she checks.

I focus on her words, trying to decode their

meaning. It's all so cryptic, leading me to believe she *does* know about Dimitri and Bram and them installing me as a spy. Or at the very least, she knows they'll have one and has assumed it's me.

"No."

"Typical men." She shakes her head and gives a wry smile. "I'm a Madam."

I blink a few times as I try to process what she's saying. Is her profession a secret? And what does it have to do with me?

"Do the people here know?" I ask.

"They didn't do a good job at briefing you, did they?" she muses.

"This is the first time they've gotten someone into one of these parties," I admit.

"Ah. That explains a lot."

Okay. So she definitely knows something.

"This is a dangerous game you're playing," she warns me.

"In general, or talking to you?" I retort.

Catherine takes out her hip flask again and pours herself another shot of blood. "Are you sure you don't want some?"

"I don't take blood from strangers," I point out. Though the point is moot when I'm basically admitting to being here illegally.

"That's wise." Instead of knocking it back, she

simply takes a sip from the glass. "I suspect the reason they didn't tell you about that fan is because they don't know much."

"Then why give it to me?"

She opens her clutch again and digs around in it before pulling out a card and handing it to me.

I take it and study the lettering.

Lady Catherine Knoylls - The Black Fan

Ah. Some of the pieces slot into place.

"So all the women with black fans in there..." I gesture vaguely in the direction of the other room.

"Work for me, yes."

"And the other colours?"

"Are women from the other upscale brothels in the city. Lord Rufus propositioned you because only women who are available for the night open their fans. Most have been to enough of these functions to recognise the girls. Lord Rufus included. But he probably hoped to try his hand at getting a cheaper price for the new girl. He won't bother you again."

"Thank you." No matter her true motives, I appreciate her rescuing me from the older vampire. "But why did you step in?"

"I've put everything I am into the Black Fan, I'm not about to let my reputation be ruined by someone sent here by an ex-priest."

My eyes widen. So she *does* know who sent me

into the city. That raises more questions than it answers, but I know better than to ask too much.

"I also have a soft spot for your employer. We've known each other a long time." She smiles fondly.

Hmm. And here's me thinking the only person who views the most powerful vampire in the country with any affection is the wife he shares with Bram.

"Thank you, whatever your reasons are," I say.

"Don't thank me yet," she warns. "It won't keep either of us alive."

It doesn't take much for me to believe her. This city is dangerous.

I fiddle with her card, only then remembering I had it. I hold it out, but she shakes her head.

"Keep it," Catherine says. "If you find yourself invited to one of these parties again, then call me. I'll be your escort and make sure no one bothers you."

"You'd do that?" It's hard to keep the disbelief out of my voice.

"As I said, I have a soft spot for your employer." She heads towards the door and swings it open. "And perhaps I don't want more blood on my hands."

A lump forms in my throat. More blood? That doesn't sound good.

"We should be getting back before anyone notices we're gone," she tells me.

I nod, knowing she's right, but not knowing what to do with myself. Of all the things that have happened since I arrived here, this conversation is right up there.

"Keep your fan closed, and if anyone asks who you are, tell them you're my newest recruit and not accepting any clients for now. It should put them off for long enough."

She's gone before I can reply, no doubt going back to the party like I should too. Not that I can bring myself to do it.

My whole body shakes, from fear or adrenaline, I'm not too sure. One of the two. But I can't stay here forever. I have to go back to the party and learn what I can, even if it's just about what to pay more attention to next time.

CHAPTER SEVEN

I push through the door to the office and make my way over to the desk. It's amazing how normal life can feel while going about my work. Almost as if I haven't spent my weekend going to deadly parties and pretending to be the newest courtesan in the city. Apparently, that's what they prefer to call themselves, and who am I to argue? Catherine is the first person to put herself in danger for me, why shouldn't I believe her?

Unless I count Bram. But I don't. He's only helping me because it's his job.

"Hey Bernice," I call, expecting the cheerful vampire I work with to respond straight away.

Silence greets me instead. I frown.

Is she on holiday? I don't remember her saying anything about it. Not that going on holiday is really a thing here. But people still take time off for family stuff, or public holidays to celebrate the greatness of the city, or something like that. I'm honestly not too sure because I haven't been here long enough.

I'm sure she'll tell me all about whatever it is she's doing once she's back. It's nothing to worry about.

Except that here, there's always something to worry about. In the worst-case scenarios, she's dead already. Or worse, being tortured. Potentially even because of me.

No. That's not going to be the case. they wouldn't have wasted time going for my workmate when I'm as easy to get to.

I try to push her disappearance from my mind. If I don't want to get fired, then I have to do my work. All I need to do is send her a quick email and then wait for her to respond.

With that decided, I type out a quick message, making sure to phrase it as if I need to know what work she needs covering while she's out of the office. If something bad has happened to her, then no one reading this will think we're in cahoots about anything. No matter how much trouble she's possibly in, I must keep my name clean. If not, it won't take long for my whole life to unravel.

Several hours later, the phone rings and makes me jump. It's too quiet in the office without Bernice.

She's not overly chatty, but the way her nails clack against her keyboard as she types has become a constant backdrop for me, and now it's gone, I find I miss it.

"Good evening, how can I help you?" I ask in my best customer voice after picking up the receiver.

Nobody answers.

"Hello? Sir? Madam? The line is bad. If you wouldn't mind calling back, I can see to your inquiry." The line isn't bad as far as I can tell. Which means someone has called me with the intention of not speaking.

I wait a moment to see if they'll say anything. Nerves make me shift uncomfortably in my seat. What is this about? And is it linked to Bernice's disappearance? I don't see how it can be, but stranger things have happened in my life.

"I'm sorry, but I can't hear you. I'm going to put the phone down now. If you call back, hopefully, the line will be better." My voice shakes, betraying how off-putting the phantom phone call is to me.

I need to pull myself together.

Not for the first time, I start questioning why they said yes to me becoming the spy in the City Of Blood. I know they were running out of options, but surely no one would be better than the sack of nerves I'm turning into. I shouldn't have volunteered for the position either. This is as much on me as Dimitri and whoever else helps him run the vampire den. Until I did that, none of them had any idea who I was. I should have kept it that way.

I turn my attention back to the work I should be doing. There are client campaigns which need to be checked and updated. It may be part of my cover in the city, but the work I do here is very real, and not doing it could result in me losing my job. That won't be a problem for me, as my rent and food are all paid for by the vampire den, but that'll raise questions from the people around me.

And give me less ins on what's happening in the city. Bernice has been a good source of what's going on since the start.

An email notification pops up on the bottom of my screen. I'm not managing to get anything else done, and it could be something urgent from one of our clients. That's enough to make me click on it.

My heart sinks as I read the bold letters at the top of the page. There's going to be another cage fight. Tomorrow.

I don't need to check my secret phone to know the others will have gotten this too. Or that they'll want me to go. I have to. And this time, I need to get proof that the city is doing something illegal. It's dangerous, but that's what I signed up for.

Wanting to make sure I haven't missed anything, I scroll down the rest of the email, scanning the text for anything of interest. The first few lines are nothing more than the time and the address, as if it changes each time. The fights are always in the same place. They're only a secret to people living *outside* the city. No one within the walls cares enough to even try and put a stop to them. In the thirty years since the City Of Blood was founded, there hasn't been a single rebellion.

Or perhaps there has been, and the outside world never heard about it. There must be people inside the city working against it. I can't be the only one who thinks badly of the place.

I'm jarred from my thoughts by the list of names. Well, one name, about halfway down the list of dozens.

Bernice Saunders.

Like I feared, my workmate hasn't gone anywhere good.

CHAPTER EIGHT

I CAN'T BELIEVE I'm back here again. Or that I have to be. The shock of what I'm about to witness is less this time, which I suppose is a good thing, but it has the unexpected side effect of making sure I pick up on all the things I missed the last time.

A waft of stale fried food and dried sweat drifts past me, almost hiding the stench of dried blood which I can smell even in the entrance hall. I'm not sure how that's possible, given the cages are in the other room.

The blood I drank before coming curdles in my stomach. Maybe it was a bad idea to drink. I thought it might help for when the fights get going and blood gets spilt, but it's already backfiring.

I step into the queue for programs behind a vampire with bright pink hair holding the hand of a boy of around ten. He's too young to see this, I'm not sure why she thinks it's a good idea to bring him here. But it isn't my place to say anything. She's his mother, it's her choice.

"Doesn't it make you hungry?" someone says behind me.

I glance over my shoulder but can't work out who said it. At least they aren't talking to me. Hungry is the *last* thing I feel when I'm in this place. I'm more likely to lose my dinner than drink more.

The woman and child step away, and I pay for my program, then take it over to the same chair I used last time. I place the booklet on my knee and lock my fingers together over the top of it, not bringing myself to open it and feel the glossy pages between my fingers. I'm not sure which bit I find worse. That the cage fights happen at all, or that they try to dress it up as if it's something special and exciting.

No wonder there used to be a vampire hunting guild. If this was how the majority of vampires used to behave, I'd have joined it myself if I'd ever been human.

Steeling my nerves, I finally open the program. It only takes me a moment to find Bernice. Her photo looks up at me with perfect hair, and a smile that says she's ready to take on the world. I'm not close to her by any stretch of the imagination, but I don't want to see what's going to happen to her next.

The echoing sound of the first fight bell rings through the entrance hall, causing a mass exodus of the people around me.

I repress a sigh and get to my feet, determined to join them no matter how much I hate what's going to happen next. This is where I need to be, and what I need to get evidence of. Ideally, I need to get myself into a position where I can take a video of something illegal happening. The only problem is that I'm not sure I'm going to be able to do it when the time comes.

The crowd jostles against me as I use them to shield me from any prying eyes. I don't think I've done anything to gain unwanted attention, but it's better to err on the side of caution.

As I pass into the room where the fights themselves happen, the stench of dried blood almost overpowers me. Unwittingly, I glance over to the cage. Dark red patches litter the floor, standing out against the older puddles of brown. No doubt that's the blood from when I was here before. Or they have private fights. That wouldn't surprise me. Especially if they look at it like a sport.

Another bell sounds, louder this time. I search for it but can't find anything.

"The fight is about to begin. All betting is now to cease," the automated voice announces. Her tinny voice is almost reassuring in the madness.

Almost.

A lone figure is pushed into the cave. She stumbles forward, then stands lost in the middle of it. She looks up, and it feels as if she meets my gaze. Her eyes questioning why she's here, and what I did to betray her.

Bernice.

I know I'm putting emotions on her that don't necessarily exist. Especially as the room is chock full of people, and I'm in the middle. She likely doesn't even realise I'm here. But knowing that doesn't stop me from feeling like she's accusing me of something.

The collar of my jumper constricts me, and I reach up to pull it away from my neck.

It's all in your mind, Chloe.

Somehow, I don't think my own reassurances are going to achieve anything. Not tonight.

Another vampire is let into the cage, but he doesn't act like all the other people I've seen in his position. He lifts his arms and screams at the crowd. They shout and cheer.

He reminds me of a gladiator from the history books, someone who revels in the death and gore of his sport.

I wish I knew anyone here well enough to ask about him, especially as I don't want to draw attention to myself by looking at my program. I should have checked who was going to be in the first fight before I came in here, but I was too focused on how I was feeling.

That's selfish, I know that now.

"He's my favourite," a woman behind me says.

"You've seen him before?" another one answers.

"Oh, yes. This is his tenth fight," the first one responds eagerly. "He's been brutal in all of his others."

Someone jostles into the back of me, but I right myself without complaining. I'm more interested in hearing more about from the women. Poor Bernice doesn't stand a chance, especially not with this being the brute's tenth fight. He's easily twice her size, and if what Vinnie told me is true, then he thinks he's going to get to go free after this.

"They should have at least made this one difficult for him," the second woman pouts. "There isn't even a challenge here."

"I know. it'll be over in seconds."

I step away, unable to stomach more of the conversation. So it's common knowledge that the victors of ten fights go free, and yet no one questions when they don't. I suppose it's safer to keep your head down and never bring up things like that, and most people want to stay alive. Especially here.

"Fight! Fight! Fight!" the crowd roars. They're more into this one than they were the previous time I was here. Could it be a different crowd, or is it because of the male vampire in the cage?

Bernice shivers, not making a move to do anything, never mind defend herself.

The brute circles her, as if trying to work out what her strategy is. He's going to be disappointed that she doesn't have one. She's nothing more than a marketing assistant who likes egg salad sandwiches and AB positive blood. Not together, though. That would be a disgusting combination.

A loud clatter draws my attention and I notice a long spear landing between Bernice and the man in the cage with her. I've never seen them do that before. Then again, I suppose the aim of the game is to entertain the masses in the bloodiest way possible, not just to kill people.

She stares at it for a moment, but then things seem to slot into place. Faster than the brute can manage, she darts forward and scoops it up. She has the advantage in being better fed, even if he doesn't seem any weaker for it. She holds the spear up in front of her, but clearly doesn't know how to hold it.

I wonder if they disclosed the spear to all the

people who placed bets against her. I hope not. If she wins, a lot of people will be out of money, which is the least they deserve.

The brute is clearly confused by what to do now she has a sharp weapon, and then charges her. Bernice doesn't even step back, she just holds her spear steady and closes her eyes.

I follow suit, squeezing my own shut as tightly as they'll go. The action seems to heighten my other senses, meaning I hear the squelch of the spear as it penetrates his body, and can smell the fresh blood.

Nausea runs through me, and I know it's only a matter of time before I get a second look at the contents of my stomach.

The crowd cheers, and the desire to know what's happening is too great to keep my eyes closed any more. I open them to find three vampires being let into the cage, each of them wearing what looks like chainmail.

Bernice's spear is going to be useless against that.

A loud clang fills the air, even over the voices of the crowd. It seems Bernice has realised the same thing I have and has dropped the spear. She puts her hands out in front of her and walks backwards, shaking her head as her lips move. I can almost hear her pleas over the din and despite the distance.

A lone tear rolls down my cheek. I wipe it away before anyone can notice.

The moment the three vampires corner Bernice, I know it isn't going to end well for her. A small part of me is screaming to rush forward and help her, but the rest is squashing that down. Not only is there nothing I *can* do, but interfering will mean I die too. And, while my life isn't worth any more or less than anyone else's, I do have an opportunity to help a lot of other people.

A male vampire twice her size opens his mouth wide, his fangs glinting in the dim light of the cage. We don't normally feed on other vampires because it doesn't do much for us nutritionally, but he must be hungry enough to try it anyway.

I gag, my hand flying to my mouth to hold in anything that may want to escape. There's a good chance I'm going to lose all the food I've eaten today.

The moment he sinks his teeth into her throat and rips it out, I know I have to get out of here. Blood gushes from the wound, falling to the floor. Sound warps and it's almost as if I can't hear a thing.

I turn around and push my way through the crowd, no longer caring if anyone is watching me. I can't deal with this any longer. Selfishly, I can't watch her die. It's so much harder when it's someone

I know. When I know things that aren't in her fighter profile in the cage fight program.

And I can't do it.

I don't know if I can even stay in the City Of Blood. But what choice do I have? Getting me in was easy, but escaping? That isn't the kind of thing people do very easily. In the past year, there are only a dozen people who have successfully gotten out. Unless they're under exaggerating the number to get me to stay, but I don't think so. Everything else they told me was an attempt to *stop* me from coming here. They only want people who are certain about it to come into such danger.

The crowd parts easily for me, and I'm out in the entrance hall with all the vendors again within moments. None of them pay me any attention, and the scent of greasy fried stuff overpowers me, doing wonders to settle my stomach.

I make my way over to the benches and drop down onto one. I resist covering my face in my hands, not wanting to draw any more attention to myself. If anyone asks, I'll say the crowd has made me too hot. I'm sure most people will realise it's a lie, but no one will really question it either.

"Is this seat taken?" a smooth male voice asks.

I glance up, keeping my surprise off my face.

Which is difficult, considering the man in front of me is as human as they come.

"Yes." Something compels me to say it, though I'm not sure exactly *what*.

He sits next to me and stretches out his legs, taking his time in saying whatever it is he came over to. I'm sure he has a purpose, and it probably isn't to turn me over to the authorities. Humans don't get the same advantages as vampires do for the information.

"Did it get too hot in there?" he asks.

I startle. How has he guessed the lie I want to use?

"Far too hot," I mumble.

He nods. "It does for me too. Every time I come back, I forget how hot the crowds make me. Something about their excitement must make things so much hotter than normal."

"Maybe it's all the metal."

The man chuckles. "Perhaps. Or maybe the dead's blood runs hot."

"Hmm."

It hasn't escaped my notice that he hasn't supplied me with a name or asked for mine.

"Sometimes, I wonder what it would be like if I was the only person in that room," he says.

"You'd want a private cage fight?" I grimace, not liking the idea in the slightest.

"Oh, no. There wouldn't be anyone in the cage."

"Ah."

Is he saying he doesn't want there to be cage fights anymore? Or am I reading too much into it? There's no real way of telling without outright asking him. But a popcorn vendor across the room has taken a sudden interest in us. We should be careful not to prolong our conversation for much longer.

"I want that too," I admit softly.

"I thought so."

I don't respond to that, waiting for him to get to the point. He's a human at a vampire event, there must be a reason for that.

"I know other people who want that too," he says. "They would like to meet someone like you."

Is he talking about some kind of resistance? I've always assumed one existed, but I haven't heard any hints of it until now. Of course, I may be wrong and reading too much into what he's saying. At this point, I may simply *want* there to be a resistance so I can feel like someone is doing something about the brutality in the city.

"That's interesting."

"If you decide you want to meet them, then you know where to find me," the man says.

"I do?"

He gets to his feet and gives me a curt nod before walking off.

All right, then. I'm going to take that as meaning he'll be here at the next cage fight. The way things are going, perhaps I will be too.

A cheer sounds from inside the room, and my stomach flips in response. I don't think I can stand spending the rest of my night watching this barbarism. Especially not when I know some of the blood now decorating the cage belongs to Bernice.

I rise to my feet and hold my head high as I walk out of the arena. No matter what happens, I won't give anyone watching a chance to see me as weak. Especially not if they belong to the resistance.

CHAPTER NINE

As soon as my alarm goes off, I click on the app which will open the blinds just enough to let in some air, but not enough for any remnants of the sun to reach in and burn my skin. I love the feel of fresh air brushing against my skin too much to leave them closed until I have to. I wish I could open them further, but I can't risk it. At least there isn't long until the evening siren, then I can open them completely.

I stretch out my arms and legs, loosing the sleep from my body. My eyes sting, reminding me I haven't had enough sleep. Just like I haven't every other night since the last cage fight.

If I'm honest about it, I haven't been sleeping well since the first one. All I see when I close my eyes is someone dying. Sometimes, it's Bernice. Others it's people I pass in the street. One time, it was me. All of it horrifying, and none of it helping me get any rest.

How can people do that to one another? I can almost understand punishing people, but why do it so publicly? Does it really stop people from revolting against the Mayor? I can't see how. Surely it has the opposite effect.

But I know that isn't true. I've seen vampires cheering, betting, and eating away while people get slaughtered in front of them.

The more I think about it, the less I want to be part of it all. It's hard to remember that's why I'm here in the first place. I'm going to get the proof they need to bring this place down. I have to.

But is that all I can be doing? Collecting information is hardly an active role in pulling down a city-state like this. And the man at the cage fight's words keep running around my mind along with the dreams. The more I think about them, the more certain I am that his talk was of the resistance.

Even if they're only making a small difference, they're doing something. And the people I've heard of who have left the City Of Blood must have gotten out somehow. Perhaps it's down to them getting them out. In which case, I should be doing everything possible to help them. It's a no brainer for me.

So why am I debating whether I should go back to try and meet him?

My alarm sounds again, alerting me that it's time to get up if I want to make the most of my time to go outside. I've heard a lot of humans say they like long lie-ins, but I don't see the appeal. Then again, there are twenty-four hours in their days when they can go outside. For me, it can be as long as sixteen and as little as two. Particularly in the summer, I like to make the most of the time I have.

Though with the outside as dangerous as it is right now, I may start rethinking that.

I swing my legs out of bed and grab my dressing gown, wrapping it around me against the chilly air. It shouldn't be this cold at this time of year, but then, that's the British weather. I wouldn't be surprised if we have a heatwave in December at some point.

The apartment is cold and empty without anyone else here. I wish I could have a pet but understand why I can't. Perhaps when I finish my assignment here, I'll get one.

If I'm still alive.

Within ten minutes, I'm sitting on the small sofa with two mugs and a plate of eggs on toast. I pick up the blood one first and swallow it down. It refreshes me instantly, and I feel alive and raring to go. The coffee will help with that too, and I completely understand the human obsession with the stuff. I flick on the TV, hoping to catch up on some of the news. Not that it'll be very much. The only things reported on here are events inside the city walls. Or those they deem too important to keep away from the general populace. It's dreadfully dull most days, but better than being taken by surprise by something.

I'm halfway through my plate of eggs when the siren finally sounds. I'm on my phone within seconds, then remember it's always best to wait ten minutes before doing anything. As much as I long to look outside, I wouldn't put it past the esteemed Mayor to do something like play the dusk siren ten minutes early just so some people die.

Regularly reminding people that they can die seems to be the way she likes to go.

Yet another reason she must be stopped.

The mere idea of joining some kind of resistance is almost enough to make me leave the building right now and go in search of the man from outside the fights. But I know it's foolish to. I don't know enough about him to even start looking, which means it'll only waste the precious time I have. I need to spend my day finding out more about the city and how it works. That's my main objective, and it's best I don't forget it.

Instead of rushing out the door, I finish my eggs, then take my plate to the kitchen. I wash it along with my mugs, bouncing up and down at the prospect of having a day to myself, even if it is one I'm going to spend sleuthing.

As I turn to hang up my tea towel, a small card on the fridge catches my eye. I move the magnet off it and study the words written in swirly font.

Catherine.

She seems like the kind of woman who knows a lot about the inner workings of the city. Perhaps she'll know something about the resistance and can point me in the right direction. Even if she doesn't, I'm sure she'll have *something* interesting to tell me.

With my mind made up, I head back to my bedroom to get dressed. Now I have a destination in mind, there's nothing that can stop me from leaving the apartment.

CHAPTER TEN

I DOUBLE AND triple check the map on my phone, wanting to be certain I'm going in the right direction. I'm surprised the brothel is on the map at all, but apparently, they're commonplace here.

The black fan hanging above the door like a pub sign gives it away the moment I'm in the street with the brothel. Other than that, it's disappointingly underwhelming and looks like every other building in the neighbourhood. They're on the larger side, and it isn't completely clear which buildings are housing, and which have businesses. According to my map, there's a dentist, doctor, and a cobbler, all practising on this street. Along with the brothel. It's an odd combination. If they're all still in business.

I stride forward and push open the door to the Black Fan. A small bell tinkles, announcing my arrival to the woman behind the desk. She's wearing a comfy but sleek black dress, with her hair tied back, and big black jewels around her neck and in her ears. She's somehow exactly what I expect someone working as a vampire courtesan to look like, and not at the same time.

"Good evening, welcome to the Black Fan, how can I help you?" she asks politely, flashing pearly white teeth at me when she smiles.

"I'm...err...here to see Catherine," I stammer out, only realising in hindsight that I should have called to check if the Madam is seeing anyone.

Should I offer to pay for her time? I don't think so. She'll dislike that.

"Do you have an appointment?" she asks.

I shake my head. "But I can make one now, if that's better."

The woman's gaze travels up and down my body, taking in my well-worn jeans and plain shirt. I've never felt so underdressed in my life.

"That won't be necessary. If you go through to the waiting room, I'll let Lady Catherine know she has a visitor." She clicks on something behind the desk, and it's only then I realise it's a tablet of some kind. They've done well to create a place away from time here.

"Thank you."

She gestures me through a curtained door, and I go into the other room. If I felt underdressed before, it's nothing compared to how I feel now. The whole room is decked out in red and black, with dripping crystals and inviting looking chairs. It easily makes me feel out of place.

But I can't just stand in the middle and wait, so I choose one of the seats and settle myself into it, waiting for Catherine to arrive and trying to collect my thoughts until then. I need to work out what I really want to ask her about the resistance. And if that's even the real reason I'm here. A small part of me is wondering if I simply want someone who I can call a friend by my side.

She sweeps into the room barely five minutes after me, her impressive dress sweeping out behind her. It's cut in the same style as the one she wore at the party, and while I can tell this one is less ornate, I can't put my finger on why that is.

"Welcome, Chloe. I thought it might be you when Sonia said I had a visitor," she says, a warm smile spreading over her face. At least she isn't annoyed by my visit, though I have no idea how I'd be able to tell. Her profession no doubt means she's more adept at lying than most people,

"Sorry, I should have given my name."

Her laugh fills the room, light and airy. It must be

fake. I can see how men would line up for days to hear that in response to one of their jokes.

"No need for anything like that here. We're a brothel, Chloe, we're more than used to people not wanting to reveal certain information."

She sits in the seat opposite me and presses the table.

I frown, trying to work out what she's done.

"I'm letting the kitchen know to bring out refreshments," she says, answering my unspoken question.

"Can't you just ask them to?"

"In front of you, perhaps. But all the tables in the public areas of my establishment have them. It's all about the illusion of effortlessness."

"Like the tablet hidden behind the fancy desk?" I nod back towards the reception.

"Exactly like that."

A girl comes over to the table with a pitcher of water and two glasses. She sets it down on the table, then disappears again. I can see how if we were deeper in conversation, she'd simply disappear into the background.

Catherine pulls her skirts to the side and shuffles forward in her seat to pour us drinks.

"Do you always wear dresses like that?" I blurt. She looks like she's stepped out of a period drama, it can't be comfortable to be wearing so many layers and fancy items all the time. I'm certain parts of her dress aren't even functional.

She chuckles as she hands me one of the glasses of water. "Just how young are you?"

A blush rises to my cheeks and I glance away to try and cover it up. I know better than to question something like that. I'm more or less asking her how old she is.

"I thought so." Catherine sighs. "Get back to me in five hundred years with what you're wearing day to day. Maybe then you'll understand what it's like to watch time pass. You'll want to cling on to your past too."

My eyes widen. Five hundred years? She barely looks older than twenty. Though that is normal for a vampire, and having grown up in a den, I should be used to it.

"I'm sorry, I'm not sure what made me ask," I admit.

She flashes me a reassuring smile, then picks up her water and takes a sip. "It isn't anything to be sorry for. I don't imagine many vampires in Dimitri's den dress like they're from a different century."

My eyes widen at her mention of his name. It's not that I'm surprised she knows it, I already suspected as much. But using it seems dangerous.

Amusement dances in her eyes. "This place is completely safe," she assures me. "I have it checked for bugs several times a day. You can speak freely here. Though you should work on keeping your thoughts to yourself. The Mayor is well aware of who Dimitri is, and I have no doubt she knows he wants to bring down her city. If someone asks about him, you need to keep a straight face."

I nod. "I'm sorry, you took me off guard."

Catherine snorts. "Any inquisitor worth his job title will try and get you to admit to things before you're taken in for questioning."

Embarrassment flares up within me. Of course that's the case. I'm not sure why I thought differently. It's foolish of me and is how I'm going to get myself killed.

"I have to admit to being impressed too," Catherine muses. "I've never encountered one of Dimitri's spies before. You're not the kind of vampire I'd expect him to send."

"The others weren't anything like me."

"So there were others." She taps a finger against her leg, as if mulling over what I'm saying.

"About half a dozen before me. We assume all of them are dead. Most were big burly guys..."

"And conspicuous as a result," Catherine finishes for me. "That's what I would have expected from

Dimitri and his advisers. Which means they either had someone change their mind, or they ran out of other people to send."

I glance at the floor, not wanting to admit how right she is about the last part. "A bit of both," I say sheepishly.

"Stands to reason." She leans back in her chair. "But you didn't come here to be lectured to about your job, I'm sure that happened enough before you came here."

I chuckle nervously. She has no idea how right she is on that front. The training to get here was some of the most intense I've ever experienced in my life.

"No, I didn't."

"Are you being sent to another of the Mayor's parties? I haven't had my invitation yet." Her thoughtful expression turns serious. She probably fears not having gotten one. I can't imagine what that might mean for someone like here.

"No, it isn't that. It's something someone said to me at one of the cage fights I had to go to." I hope she picks up on how little I wanted to be at them. But she's a smart woman, she'll pick up on that.

"And what was that?" She sits forward in her chair, waiting for what I'm going to say next.

"He didn't outright say it, but I think he was talking about the resistance. He said..."

"Don't go near them," she warns darkly.

"So they're real?" My heart thuds in my chest, excitement growing within me.

"Yes. There's a resistance in the city." Something about the way she says it makes me feel as if there's more to it than she's saying.

Ways to get her to tell me more start flitting through my mind.

"Where can I find them?" I ask.

"You don't." Catherine's expression remains stern. "If they want someone, they approach them. But if they do that to you, then you have to say no, Chloe. The resistance is dangerous."

"Because they're managing to change things?" I ask hopefully, even though I'm reasonably certain I know what the answer is.

"The only thing they ever manage to do is get people killed. And you'll be one of them if you let them recruit you. It's one of the fastest ways to get killed in the city."

I snort. "I thought that was just living here," I mutter.

To my surprise, Catherine laughs. "You have a point. Even breathing is dangerous here. But please, believe me when I say the resistance is bad news.

They're heading in a direction which will get them all killed, and innocent people along with them."

A lump forms in my throat, and I swallow it down, hoping to hide my nervousness. But with someone as good with people as Catherine is sitting next to me, that's nearly impossible.

"Promise me you won't take the risk?" Catherine begs.

I'm surprised by the earnestness of her plea, even if I'm not sure where it comes from. Is it worry for me? Or how it will reflect on her?

"I promise." Even as the words leave my mouth, I know they're a lie. I don't plan on running off and signing up right now, but if the opportunity comes knocking, I'm not sure I can say no. Not when I could make such a difference to the people in the city.

Catherine sighs in relief and finally relaxes. "Thank you."

I push away the guilt threatening to overtake me. When it comes down to it, I have a job to do. One that may involve breaking my promise if I'm ordered to.

Or if I feel like it's the right thing to do. I'm not sure I can sit back and watch more people die if I'm given a chance to stop it.

CHAPTER ELEVEN

Rain pounds on the pavement the moment I leave the office. It's always the case. The moment I no longer have to be inside, the weather turns miserable. It shouldn't be this gloomy in June.

The door swings shut behind me, letting me distance myself from my fake job and the frustrations it brings, which are very real. I must admit, I never thought about the consequences of having to have two jobs at the same time. Especially when I can't get fired from one for the sake of the other.

I bow my head and start to walk away as quickly as I can. The sooner I get home, the sooner I'll be able to get out of my soaking clothes and into the shower. After that, I'll have to work out what the best use of my time is. I hope the weather gets better, the rain makes it difficult to investigate anything, especially as there isn't anyone on the streets.

As if summoned by my thoughts, a shadowy figure catches my eye. I glance up, but no one is there. I'm getting paranoid and need to be careful not to let it affect my judgement.

A chill wind joins the rain, causing a shiver to run down my spine. I pull my jacket closer to me, glad I thought to bring it, even if it isn't as waterproof as I'd like it to be right now.

"Hello, Chloe," a familiar voice says.

I whip my head up to find the man from the cage fights leaning against the wall up ahead. I glance around, checking to see if there's anyone else around. While there's no rule against spending time with one another, most vampires and humans stick to their own kind. It creates less complications. And most of the humans are up and about during the sunlit hours, particularly in the summer. It's safer for them that way. Though technically it's illegal for a vampire to kill a human, I doubt they'd be punished if they did.

"The coast is clear," the man says. "I already checked."

"You'll have to forgive me if I want to make sure of that myself," I respond curtly.

"Don't you trust me?" A wide grin takes over his

face, giving him a more boyish edge than he's had previously. Which is surprising, considering he looks to be about my age.

"Why would I do that? You've cornered me outside work in the pouring rain and not explained how or why you know my name." I cross my arms, wincing at the wet squelch of my jacket. I need to get a waterproof one that's lightweight enough for summer if this weather continues.

I brush back a strand of hair that's started to clump on my forehead, annoyed that the rain only seems to be making the human look better, while I get progressively more bedraggled.

"I see your point. But you should trust me. You haven't been arrested yet." He shrugs as if that's proof of anything.

"It's hard to be arrested when I've done nothing wrong," I bluff, proud of how steady my voice is, especially when I keep cracking in front of Catherine.

He steps closer to me and leans in, his lips inches away from my ear. "We both know that isn't true," he whispers.

I scowl and step back. "That's a heavy accusation to throw at someone."

His impish grin returns. "Have you thought about meeting with the people I told you about?"

"I have." And I still haven't made up my mind, something I'm not about to admit to him.

"And?"

"What's in it for me?" I raise my chin and flash him the most defiant look I can.

"A chance to make a difference."

They're dangerous. Catherine's voice rings through my mind. Though there is a chance he isn't talking about the resistance at all, and I'm simply being over-cautious about the whole thing.

"I can take you there now, if you want to," he suggests as he slips his hands into his pockets.

Headlights flash against the side of a building in front of me, and the two of us freeze in position, waiting to see if we need to hide so the car can go past without raising any suspicion about us. One thing is for sure, having a conversation with a stranger in the pouring rain is a good way to look guilty.

I hold my breath, only letting go of it when the lights fade and the car heads down a street that isn't ours. We're safe. For now. We need to get out of the open soon, or we were going to end up attracting the wrong sort of attention.

Why am I thinking of us as a unit already when I don't know anything about him?

"I still don't know your name," I blurt.

"No, you don't."

"Are you going to tell me it now?"

"That depends if you'll agree to come with me," he returns smoothly.

I raise an eyebrow. "How am I to even know if the name you give me is real? For all I know, you'll give me a fake one."

"That's why we'll only use our forenames."

A snort escapes me before I can stop it. "Are you trying to tell me you know my first name, and where I work, but you don't know my surname? I'm sorry, but I don't believe it." I unfold my arms and place my hands on my hips, staring him down. If he thinks I'm some kind of wilting flower, then he has a hard lesson to learn. I may not be doing a good job of holding my lunch down at cage fights, but that doesn't mean I'm a pushover.

"Fair point. But I promise I'm the only one who knows it." He holds up his hands in the universal term of surrender.

I narrow my eyes as I try to get a measure of him, but it impairs my vision too much with the rain.

"All right. Fair is fair. I'm Oscar Bell."

"That sounds like a fake name," I counter.

He shrugs. "I can show you my ID if you want."

"Because they can't be faked," I quip, thinking of my own stash hidden back at the apartment. I haven't had a reason to use one of them yet, but I have no doubt they'll pass even the most rigorous of inspections. No doubt any fake ones he has will too.

"So, are you going to come with me?" he asks.

I consider for a moment, weighing up everything I know about him. There's a chance this could be some kind of elaborate trap, but I don't think so. It's my job to find out as much information about the city as possible, and can I really do that without learning about the resistance? If that's the case, then I *have* to say yes to him.

Besides, it's only a meeting. What harm can come from that? So long as I don't sign up to do anything before I can talk to one of my employers about it.

"Yes, I'll come with you," I say after a moment.

His grin spreads wider. "You won't regret it."

No, Oscar, I hope I won't.

CHAPTER TWELVE

The building in front of us has seen better days, even without the rain.

"Where are we?" I ask Oscar, hoping he hasn't lured me here in order to kill me, or something like that.

He's human, he can't do that. And not just because it's illegal. Even drenched to the bone and colder than I want to be, I have the edge when it comes to speed and strength. If he wants to take me on, then he'll have a fight on his hands.

"This is the centre of the resistance," he says, gesturing towards the front door.

I grimace and nod in what I hope appears like an enthusiastic manner. I'm not feeling it, though. Nothing about this building fills me with confidence about the kind of operation the resistance is running. Perhaps Catherine is right and the only thing they're going to be able to achieve is getting themselves killed.

I shouldn't make assumptions based on appearance. I don't want them to do the same to me just because I'm a vampire, or because I'm female. That's been done to me enough while training to become a vampire agent. So many of the bigger, bulkier men dismiss me out of hand because I'm slight.

"Are we going inside?" I ask instead of voicing any of my inner opinions.

He nods. "If you want to."

"I do." I've come this far, there's no backing out now.

Without saying another word, he leads me through the front door and into the place which houses the people making the biggest difference in the city.

The moment I'm inside, I realise how wrong I am about the condition of the building. Everywhere I look, there's fancy equipment, some of which must have been smuggled in from outside the city, a feat that's impressive on its own.

Oscar chuckles as he takes in my expression. "The outside is kept like that on purpose. As far as the authorities know, this place is an old apartment block for humans and was cleared out five years ago in one of the Mayor's purges." His upper lip curls into a snarl as he says the last bit. A sentiment I can completely agree with. I wasn't in the city then, but I've heard horror stories. Even Bernice has some.

Had. She's gone now. She won't be telling me anything about her life ever again. Pain lances through me, but I push it away. I have to focus on what's in front of me and finding out as much as I can.

"Would you like a tour?" he asks after giving it a moment to sink in.

"Please." I couldn't ask for a better opportunity. Perhaps I'll learn everything I need to in this one trip and no one will need me to go near the resistance ever again.

Except for me. I must remember my own emotions count. I can't compromise who I am for someone else, and I'm growing more determined by the day that the City Of Blood needs to fall. At the moment, I think my best shot is to carry out my recon work and report back. The vampires on the outside can then make a plan to tear down the walls.

But all of that can change. Sometimes, controversial actions are needed to break the abusive patterns.

"What's done out of here?" I ask Oscar.

"Everything. As far as I know," he admits.

"You're not sure?" Interesting. That means he

probably isn't the one who decided to bring me in.

"No one is sure of everything. That's how we maintain our secrets."

"But isn't it dangerous to have so many people know where your centre of operations is?" I ask as we pass yet another resistance member. By my count, that's at least two dozen members. The human-vampire split is about half and half from what I've seen so far. Which makes sense to me. The city is bad no matter which side of that divide you are. Though I imagine there's more humans involved who are currently sleeping. And it'd be foolish to have everyone under one roof at the same time. I'm both surprised and relieved by the number of people that must mean they're working together.

He directs me down a corridor, and I turn while I wait for him to answer.

"Perhaps. But no one has revealed it yet."

"Hmm." It feels reckless to me. Especially bringing an unknown element into the fold like me. They know next to nothing about me. And if they know I'm a spy, even for someone who'd work with them, then they wouldn't have brought me with them.

"You don't think we're making the right decision?" he asks.

"It feels risky. All it'll take is one person being

tortured and the whole operation will be compromised," I point out.

"That's why we teach our people the best way to end their lives if they're captured," a woman says from behind us.

I turn around to find a middle-aged human with a short black bob and glasses looking at me with interest.

"Is this the girl you told us about?" she asks Oscar.

"Yes, ma'am." He stands up straighter, and I'm almost surprised he doesn't salute too.

"With all due respect, I'm a woman not a girl." I hold my head up high. I haven't been a girl in a long time.

"You barely look eighteen," she says, dismissing me again.

I bite my lip to stop from informing her I'm twenty-seven, and that I'm sure she knows how vampire ageing works. But I know it's pointless. Especially as I *do* look older than eighteen. Like most born-vampires, I stopped ageing in my early twenties, though I'm not sure of the exact point, no one has found it.

"Chloe, this is Heather, the leader of the resistance. Heather, this is Chloe. She's the one I told you about," Oscar repeats.

"Hmm." She looks me up and down, her lips pursed and disapproving. I almost think she's going to get out a tape measure and start telling me all the things she thinks is wrong with me.

I resist the urge to stand straighter. She'll come to the same conclusions no matter what I do right now.

"You've done your research on her?" Heather asks Oscar.

He nods. "Everything we're told to."

"What's her job?"

"Marketing. Low level," Oscar replies.

Should I be freaked out that he knows that? I don't think so. Not when it's easy to work out based on where I work.

"Not exactly the biggest need for us. We can't go around advertising for more recruits," she observes.

"There are ways to market on the sly," Oscar points out.

"Hmm." I can tell she isn't impressed, but I'm not sure he's cottoned on to it yet. "What makes her an asset to the resistance, other than *marketing*?" she asks him, her disdain for my fake job dripping from every word.

"You know I can speak for myself, right?" I snap, having had enough of her. Actually, of both of them.

Heather turns to me and raises an eyebrow. "Very well, then. What can you offer the resistance?"

A small part of me wants to respond by saying I'd take my services elsewhere, but I think better of it. Not only does that stop me being able to gather information, but it may affect whether they allow me to become part of the resistance in the first place. And while I may not like the woman in front of me, that doesn't mean I disagree with the cause as a whole. Far from it. I *want* to bring down the city as much as everyone else in the building does.

"That depends on what you want to achieve. But I have contacts that can get me invitations into the Mayor's parties." The words tumble out even as I'm thinking them. I have no idea if Dimitri and the others can get me another ticket, but I'm guessing so. And if not, then I may be able to get Catherine to take me with her. So long as she doesn't know who I'm going for.

Heather's eyebrows almost disappear into the fringe of her bob. "That *is* interesting."

Yes. It is. And hopefully, it will be enough for her to stop dismissing me out of hand. No matter if I have an ulterior motive or not, I am an asset to the resistance she wants.

"Fine. But you are Oscar's responsibility. If you set a foot out of line, then he will pay the consequences," Heather warns.

I want to check with him to see if he's okay with

that, but I hold Heather's gaze instead. She's the kind of woman who only responds to people she believes are her equals. And while I'm not sure I'm that, I know how to make my mark on her.

"You have a mission on Tuesday evening. Make sure she's prepped," she barks at Oscar, then turns on her heels and walks off, leaving the two of us alone.

"So that's the leader of the resistance," I mutter. She isn't very likeable. Though I'm not sure I'd expect someone in her position to be. She'll have to make too many decisions about putting people in danger to be friendly towards the people below her.

"The one and only."

"She's something else."

Oscar laughs nervously and runs his hand across the back of his neck. "I hope she hasn't put you off."

"Off from what? No one's actually asked me if I want this," I point out.

His face drains of colour, no doubt as he realises he's skipped a step in the signing me up process.

I place a hand on his arm and smile reassuringly. "It's fine. Don't worry. I've wanted this for a while." And just like that, I'm part of the resistance, even if I said I was going to wait until I had proper orders about it.

Part of being undercover is being able to go with the flow sometimes. Which means we're all going to have to deal with the new development and what it means for the rest of my mission. Hopefully, it won't be anything bad.

"So, she said we have a mission," I prompt.

"Oh. Right. It's just a stakeout. Nothing very interesting."

I shrug. "Anything that helps, right?"

"That's definitely the right attitude to have. When I signed up, I thought it was going to be all action, all the time. But mostly it's waiting," Oscar says.

It sounds a lot like being a spy. I wish I could share the thought with him. I think he'll find it amusing. But I know I can't.

He continues to chatter away happily now he knows I'm going to be a part of this. The more he does it, the more I'm reminded of the boyish smile from earlier, and I find myself smiling, wanting to encourage the charm.

The idea of spending more time with him at a stakeout sounds good to me, especially now I'm seeing a glimpse of what I suspect is the real him.

As he fills me in on everything I need to know, the reality of what's happened sinks in.

Despite my promise to Catherine, and the primary objective of my mission here, I'm now part of the resistance to bring down the City Of Blood.

CHAPTER THIRTEEN

"Where did you get this?" I ask Oscar as I run my fingers along the dashboard of the small car we're sat in. When he brought me here to start our stakeout, I didn't believe him at first.

"It belongs to my family," he answers easily. "Want a biscuit?" He holds out a packet of chocolate-covered digestives.

"Thanks." I take the top one and bite into it, wiping away the crumbs which fell on me. "It's ages since I've had one of these."

"Me too," he admits. "I save all the best snacks for stakeouts. It makes the time pass quicker. Though now I have someone to do it with, perhaps it isn't so bad."

I smile at him and lean back in my seat. It's been a

while since I've been in a car, so it's taken me a little while to get comfortable again.

"How come your family owns a car?" I ask, not wanting to let him get away with a wishy-washy answer like he's given. "I thought people didn't drive them anymore."

"Oh, nobody drives it. I'm not even sure it will work anymore."

"Then how do you move it around for stakeouts?" I don't think we'd be sitting here if it wasn't the right place to catch the man we're supposed to be watching.

"For the most part, we don't." He munches on another digestive, then offers me another one.

I take it, grateful for a small taste of home. Biscuits like this are one of the luxuries which cost a fortune inside the city. Back home, I could get a packet like this for fifty pence, but Oscar has probably paid more like three or four pounds for them. It doesn't seem like a lot at first, but it adds up, and it's more than I can justify spending while here.

"It's been here for a few years now. It just so happens that it's parked in the perfect position to watch this house." He points towards the townhouse in front of us.

The building looks as if it was built in the Victorian era, but I don't know enough about architecture to know that for sure.

"Who lives here again?" I ask, even though I know the answer already thanks to my briefing before coming here.

"Andrew Forbes. He's the Mayor's current second in command."

"I thought her second was someone-Mills?" My stomach twists into knots as I tell yet another lie. I'm well aware that Mills is no longer the second-in-command because I've met him. And not inside the city.

Oscar shakes his head, then notices a small patch of crumbs on the collar of his shirt and brushes them away. "Mills disappeared. No one knows what happened to him. He must have done something really bad for the Mayor not to want to make his execution public."

"Oh. Right. I don't watch many of the executions."

Try, I watch all of them, but with the sound turned down.

"And yet you go to cage fights," he observes.

"Only those two times," I counter. But I need to be careful. He seems to like me, but I can't reveal too much, or he'll guess that I'm not as much of an innocent bystander as I first appear.

"What made you go then?" he asks, shifting

around so he can face me.

"Don't we need to watch the house?" I ask, pointing needlessly. He's well aware of where the building is, and it's highly unlikely to move.

He shrugs and points to a small device sitting on the dashboard. "Motion sensor. It'll go off if anyone walks past. Is that your way of avoiding the question?"

Ah. Damn. He caught that.

"It isn't," I fib. "It's hard to explain." At least that's the truth.

"I've been told I'm a pretty good listener," he says.

"I'm sure you are." *But that doesn't mean I can tell you.*

I make the mistake of meeting his gaze and end up staring into his deep brown eyes. When he returns the look, I know I'm in trouble. No matter when he finds out about my real purpose here, he's going to be hurt. Truth be told, I think I will be too. I don't want to lie to him.

Stop it, Chloe. You don't even know him. If I keep reminding myself of that fact, then perhaps I'll be able to move on from him easily enough. Except that I *am* starting to know him. He likes digestive biscuits, his family own a car...

No. I have to stop.

"My friend told me about the cage fights," I

mumble. Technically true other than the friend part.

"And it made you want to go?"

I shake my head. "I needed to know if it was true." That sounds plausible to me at least.

I turn away from the intensity in his gaze and start taking in my surroundings. Bats flit between some of the trees, chirping away as they hunt for food.

"I understand needing to see it to believe it. But why go back a second time?" Oscar asks softly, as if knowing he's on shaky ground. I try not to feel too guilty about that, given that the reason isn't the one he thinks it is.

I sigh. "The friend who told me about the fights in the first place was put in one." I tuck a strand of hair behind my ear to try and distract myself from the threat of tears. Oscar barely knows me, the last thing he needs is to see me cry over my workmate.

"I'm so sorry." He reaches out and places a hand on my leg. His touch burns in the best way, even through my jeans.

To my surprise, my fangs elongate, and I find myself homing in on the sound of his heartbeat. I'm not too sure what's happening, especially when I made sure to have some blood before I came out. I didn't think it was a good idea to spend a lot of close-quarters time with a human while thirsty.

It appears I made the right decision.

"You don't have to be sorry," I say once I have my fangs back under control. I want to brush his hand away to make sure I don't feel that way again, but it seems rude to. Especially when I like the comfort it brings.

"I guess it explains why you ran out of there during that fight..."

I nod. "Why were you there?" I ask, wanting to turn his attention away from me so my lies didn't start to unravel.

He chuckles nervously. "Believe it or not, I was there to find someone like you. We're always on the lookout for new recruits to the cause. But it's hard to do when so many people will turn you in."

"Oh."

"So we watch the events like the fights for people who seem to hate it. You were exhibiting all of the signs we normally look for when we're looking for a new recruit."

"Which are?" I can't meet his eyes, and instead focus on a loose thread in the hem of my shirt. I pick at it with one of my nails.

"It's hard to explain it," he admits, leaning back in his seat. At least he's probably not thinking too much about what my nervous behaviour means then. "Most of it is body language. If you can figure out how people are expressing their true feelings, then it's easy to pick up on them. You were a tough one though. I almost didn't approach you."

I look up, my surprise too much to hide. Catherine is right, I really do need to work on my poker face. "Why did you?"

"A gut feeling," he admits. "I decided against it after seeing you back there again. Even while we were inside the arena, I kept searching for you in the crowd and deciding you weren't showing enough of what we needed. But then I saw you on the bench outside, visibly shaken, and I knew you were the kind of person who wanted to make a change." He shrugs.

"Oh."

"It sounds more insightful than it is," he promises. "And it could have gone very wrong if my first feeling had been right."

I laugh, but the sound is hollow. No doubt he was picking up on some kind of spy vibes I've been giving up. He should have passed me over. Now it's too late.

Though no matter what happens, I'm going to do everything I can to make sure he stays safe and doesn't suffer because he happened to pick the wrong person.

"So, are we expecting Forbes to do anything interesting?" I ask, desperate to change the subject.

"Sadly not," Oscar admits. "If we're on duty again with him, I can bring a pack of cards, but I didn't think about it first."

"What do you normally do while you're doing this? Maybe we can do that?"

He rubs the back of his neck again, a gesture he seems to make when he's nervous about something he has to say.

"I play games on my phone. Sometimes I read books."

"Oh? What kind?" I shuffle round in my seat, thinking this is a safe topic. Most books find their way inside the walls at some point, so anything I read before coming here should be around now.

"Do you really want to know?" he asks.

I nod. "Of course. I love to read, maybe I'll find something new."

He gives me a weak smile. "I've just finished one about a cat assassin."

"That sounds like a good combination," I muse. "Every cat I've ever met could easily have been an assassin in disguise, or a ninja." I tap a finger against my chin as I think about it.

Tension melts away from him now I'm taking him seriously.

"What about you? What was the last thing you read?" he asks.

I cast my mind back to the weeks leading up to me arriving here. I haven't had much reading time since arriving. "It was about a detective with a hellhound puppy."

"That sounds awesome."

"It was," I assure him. I need to check if the next book in the series is out, now I'm thinking about it.

"Maybe we could do a book swap and talk about them?" he suggests softly.

"I'd like that." For what feels like the first time since our stakeout started, I'm telling the truth.

No. Wait. The second time. The gratitude about biscuits was real.

"So we just sit here until dawn?" I double-check.

He nods. "Just before. I don't want to have to brush up your ashes."

Laughter bursts from me. "My ashes?"

"When you burst into flames from sun exposure." His expression is deadly serious, and I wonder why no one has ever told him what happens to vampires in the sun.

"That's not how it works," I assure him. "I could survive for a little bit but would be severely burned. Most vampires have been burned at some point or other. We all want to know what the sun looks like."

"Did you?"

"Mmhmm. I was seven, I think. Mum always told me not to go outside, but I was a kid and never listened. One day, she forgot to put the catch on the backdoor and I took my chance. I've never risked it since." I shiver at the memory of the ice bath she dumped me in.

"But it doesn't scar?" He eyes the bare skin of my throat.

"I was only outside for a minute at the most. Longer and I think it causes more damage. I think it's more severe for turned-vampires too. Or perhaps they're just more prone to wanting to see the sun one more time."

"I couldn't imagine not being able to go out during the day," he says softly.

"I don't know any different," I admit. "But from everything turned-vampires have said, the yearning to see the sun fades, but never completely goes away."

We lapse into silence, both of us consumed by our own thoughts, of which there are plenty. I need to work out how I can carry on my pretence without hurting the second person to treat me like a friend since I got here.

I fear that pain will be inevitable.

CHAPTER FOURTEEN

I DROP a basic report of the previous night's stakeout in the pile for Heather to read. Just like the other six Oscar and I have done together, nothing happened. I think we're both supposed to find it tedious, but actually, it's far from it. I enjoy spending the time with him, especially as we seem to have fallen into our groove with what to do and talk about. Including making sure we're reading the same books so we can talk about them.

I search the room for any sign Oscar's meeting with Heather is over, but I can't see him anywhere. I don't know why she didn't want me in there. Perhaps she's asking him how he thinks I'm getting on. Either that, or she's punishing me for standing up to her. I'm not sure which.

With nothing else to do, I start to walk around

the room. There's nothing of interest to either me, or my employers here, I've already discerned that much. But it doesn't matter. I have to keep busy, or I'm going to obsess over what's happening in that meeting.

Eventually, Oscar appears, walking back into the room with his head held high and a bounce in his step.

My heart skips a beat at the sight, but I push the sensation away. It's nothing but a silly schoolgirl crush, the kind I haven't had since I was at Grimalkin Academy and fancied one of the boys in my history class. The resistance against a dictatorial vampire isn't the right place for me to have a crush, even if it is on someone as charming, sweet, and intelligent as Oscar.

No. Stop it.

He waves across the room, and I return the gesture with a big smile on my face. He makes short work of the distance between us.

"Is everything all right?" I ask.

He nods. "I just got our next assignment."

"Is it an exciting one?" Given the smile on his face, it must be. Maybe we're finally going to get to do *something*. Even though I know it's safer for me and my secret if I carry on with the boring jobs, I'm finding myself wanting to do more and more as time passes. Something that isn't helped by the odd silence from Dimitri and Bram. They haven't sent me a single message in weeks, never mind any direction.

"Oh, erm. No. We've got more of the same," he admits.

I cock my head to the side. "Then why do you look like the cat who got the cream?"

A nervous smile twists at his lips, as if he's been caught with something he isn't supposed to have. The more I get to know him, the more certain I am that he's a child at heart. But the best kind. One that can be mature and sensible when he needs to be but has unbridled joy he's willing to let out when he can. He's not the kind of person I expected to meet here, but I'm glad I have. Oscar is the kind of man who can brighten up anyone's life.

"I was happy because it meant I got to spend more time with you," he admits sheepishly.

My mouth forms a small o as I think of how to respond to that. I must admit to being glad of the same thing, especially as it gives me a small reprise from some of the darker thoughts I have about this city. Ironically, he's my ray of sunshine. Or perhaps that should be moonlight.

A loud siren cuts through the air, and I jump out of my skin. At least it saves me from having to come up with a satisfactory response to Oscar's sweetness.

He puts a hand on my arm to steady me, and I flash him a grateful smile.

"What's happening?" Heather demands as she walks into the room.

"Mandatory announcement," one of the men working the computers says.

"Put it on the big screen," she orders.

He nods and clicks a few buttons until a huge screen lights up to reveal the news anchor with a grim expression on his face. I step back, bumping into Oscar's chest as I do. Instead of pushing me away, he wraps one of his arms around me, and I lean into him, enjoying the support he's giving, even if it can only be for this moment.

"Good evening," the anchor says. "I hope you're all having a splendid day. We have two special announcements at this time."

I twist around so I can share a confused look with Oscar. We haven't heard anything through the grapevine about announcements. I wonder what they are.

"First, the thirtieth anniversary parade will be taking place on the sixteenth..."

"It isn't enough time," a woman mutters from beside Heather.

"It's fine," the resistance leader responds, cutting her off.

"There will be televised executions at dusk tomorrow. This is mandatory viewing for anyone who has access to a television set," the anchor announces, keeping his face surprisingly neutral. I'm not sure how he manages to be so emotionless when it comes to reporting on upcoming deaths.

"Frederick," Heather barks at the computer man. "Find out what we can about the executions. Who, what and where. We need to know if any of our agents have been compromised."

"What happens if they are?" I whisper to Oscar.

"Then we abandon this place," Heather says coolly, eyeing me with distaste.

Oops. I'll speak quieter next time.

Before I can ask why that's necessary when she's so convinced none of her people will break and reveal the base's whereabouts, she walks off.

"I've got something," Frederick says to no one in particular. "But it isn't concrete."

"What is it?" Oscar asks, moving over to the screen so he can see what the other man can.

I hang back like the spare part I am. But that doesn't mean I'm not listening. I may need to report this back to several people, and that means paying as much attention as I can.

"Just a rumour," Frederick continues. "Apparently one of the prisoners tomorrow is from outside the walls."

My vision begins to blur as my whole world falls away. Outside the wall means someone who shouldn't have been here. Someone like Bram. Maybe that's why they haven't gotten in contact with me lately. They can't.

I'm not even sure what to do about that. Do I head underground in case he's been tortured and revealed who I am and where I live? I don't think hiding will do much in the long run, but it may buy me enough time to find a way out or create a new identity. Whichever gives me the best chance with the rebellion.

"Chloe? Are you all right?" Oscar asks.

"Oh, sorry. Yes. I think I need a drink," I lie. At least both he and Frederick are human and have no idea about how blood withdrawal works. They may fall for this lie.

I hope so, because the alternative means I'll have to admit to being here as a spy. And somehow, I don't think the resistance will take kindly to that.

CHAPTER FIFTEEN

I ALMOST DON'T TURN the TV on, but I know that isn't really an option for me. I need to know if Bram is the person from outside the city they're going to execute.

Logically, I'm aware that if my identity is known, they'd have already been over to arrest me, and I'd be sharing the metaphorical scaffold with Bram. But that doesn't settle my nerves.

Not for the first time since the announcement, I find myself longing to reach out to Oscar and ask him to come watch with me. But I know it isn't an option. If I do that, he'll know something is wrong, and press me to tell him what it is. In my current state, I may even cave and tell him.

Which means I can't ask him for help. Not this time, no matter how much I want it.

I perch on the edge of my sofa and stare at the screen. My coffee is already cold, but I'm not bothered by it. I don't think I can drink it now. The blood hasn't even made it into a mug this evening. There's no chance I can stomach it with what I'm about to watch. It's a good job I don't need daily blood to survive. It's one of those things that makes life easier but isn't necessary.

The news anchor is filling us all in on several items, none of which mean anything, and completely pale into insignificance compared to the upcoming executions. I wonder if they'll read their crimes this time. Each event like this I've forced myself to watch has been different, which doesn't help with what to expect.

The only relief is that it's scheduled for dusk and not dawn, which means it's unlikely they're going to burn any vampires to death. That's always one of the worst ones. Though I've never watched the entire thing, choosing not to traumatise myself if I don't need to.

"And now, to the main event. Our reporter is in the main square to bring you the latest news and updates about the executions. Can you hear me, Stuart?" the anchor asks.

The screen splits in two, one pane showing the

studio, and the other showing the reporter with the main square behind him.

"I can hear you loud and clear, Brian. And as you can see, I'm here in the main square waiting for the executions to begin. This will also be the stage for the celebrations and parade on the sixteenth. I can't wait for those," Stuart half-shouts into his microphone.

"Me neither," Brian admits. "It's going to be a sight to behold. I've been hearing some whispers about some of the parade details and it's going to put the twenty-five-year anniversary to shame."

"As it should," the reporter responds. "This is a big year for our esteemed leader..."

A gong sounds, and excitement fills the man's eyes.

"This is it." Stuart's eagerness comes through his voice. "The executions are about to begin."

His screen gets bigger, with Brian the anchor relegated to the corner.

I bite my bottom lip, hoping against all the odds that Bram isn't among the prisoners.

The camera pans in on five people waiting, all with bags covering their heads. Bile rises in my throat, but I manage to keep myself from throwing up. At least if I fail at that later, no one is here to see it.

"Do we know much about these executions, Stuart?" Brian asks.

The reporter shakes his head. "All we've been told is that there are five people. Four humans and one vampire, and that they're charged with breaking the laws of the city."

I scoff. As if that's a real crime. Especially when the laws change to suit the needs of the Mayor. No one can pretend she's fair minded at the best of times, and certainly not when she wants rid of someone.

Stuart presses a finger to his ear. "We're actually getting information through now," he announces. "The first traitor is Benjamina Davis."

The bag is pulled off the woman's head. She stares straight ahead with a defiant expression in her eyes. Despite the fact I don't know her, a rush of pride towards the woman. Even with death on the horizon, she wants to stick it to the city. I can respect anyone who wants to do that.

"The vampire is George Townsend. He's been charged with four counts of attempting to turn humans."

I suck in a breath. If it's true, then it explains why they're being punished together, and he's not been staked out to burn. Perhaps the four humans are ill, and he wants to save them. He wouldn't be the first vampire to do that. Or has agreed to for money or other favours. Not that it makes it any less illegal to turn them.

Technically, it's also frowned upon outside the City Of Blood too. Though they won't kill anyone for it, and if the human is dying, then it's generally considered to be acceptable.

The bag is pulled from the vampire's head and he's dragged to a post, his hands bound behind him.

"George!" Benjamina cries, trying to get to her feet, but slipping and falling.

"Mina, no!" He sounds desperate, and he stares at her as if he's about to lose the most precious thing in the world to him.

No doubt they're together.

"Let her go," he insists. "She did nothing wrong." His pleas fall on deaf ears. None of the officials are foolish enough to even respond.

Stuart introduces the other humans. Diana and Bruce, a middle-aged couple. Each of them is attached to another post, so they can see each other clearly. It's barbaric enough that they're to be executed, but they're being made to watch each other die.

I think the first person is the luckiest. They don't have to watch the others being killed in front of them.

"The final human is Hilda Davis," Stuart says as the bag is pulled off the final woman's head.

My eyes widen and my whole body turns cold. The woman is close to eighty and shaking with the exertion of what's happening.

"Grammy, Grammy, no," Benjamina screams. "You shouldn't have come."

Tears stream down my face as the pieces begin to slot into place. The old woman probably tried to sneak into the city to reunite with a granddaughter she hasn't seen since the wall went up one last time before she dies. And now it's going to cost both their lives. I'm not sure where the other couple fits into things. They're being a lot quieter than the others.

I resist the urge to turn off the TV and stop watching. These people deserve the respect of people like me, and I'm going to give it to them by watching their final moments and wishing them a swift chance at peace.

And then, I'm going to bring this city to its knees. It may take years, but I will see it burn. The resistance has me heart and soul, no matter where my other loyalties lie.

CHAPTER SIXTEEN

THE RESISTANCE HEADQUARTERS is bustling today. Which makes sense. With the thirtieth anniversary approaching, there's a lot of intelligence which needs gathering, and things put in place. The vampire elite are busier than ever too, which means those of us whose job it is to tail them are having to do more.

As much as I'm disappointed I don't have as much down time with Oscar, I'm grateful to be able to do something that makes a real difference rather than simply sitting and waiting.

"Chloe, can I have a word," Heather says, waving me over.

Butterflies take up residence in my stomach. Has she found out about my role as a spy? What will she do about it? I don't think she'll kill me, but I doubt it will go down well.

Despite my apprehensions, I follow her into the tiny room she uses as an office. It's filled with the brim with papers and maps, none of which make any sense to me. But that's fine. I'm not the one who has to decipher them.

"Is everything all right?" I ask, confused by what's going on.

"I need to talk to you about a mission," she says.

I perk up instantly. That sounds exciting.

"I thought I did all of my missions with Oscar?" I haven't seen him yet today, but I don't want to go out into the city without him. He makes me feel safe.

"They are. But this one is on the dangerous side, and I want to give everyone the individual choice about whether to take part, or stay here and hold down the fort," Heather says.

I have to give it to her, she may be stone cold and a bit of a control freak, but at least she's fair. I never feel like I'm going to be sent to do something that could get me killed. Though perhaps that's about to change now.

"All right," I acknowledge.

"Why don't you take a seat." She indicates to one of the chairs which isn't covered in papers, and I sit down.

It must be serious if she wants me to prepare for whatever it is she has to say.

"We think the time is right to attempt an assassination on the Mayor," she says simply.

"An assassination?" I repeat.

It's a bold idea, I'll give her that. One I'm not sure we have the manpower or brains to pull off. From what I've seen, the Mayor has bodyguards and protectors around her at all times. Not to mention she's a powerful vampire in her own right, and some of her followers actually believe the things she preaches, and no doubt they'd die for her.

"It's bold, I know. But with the parade coming up, I don't think there'll be a better time. She'll need to be seen during that time, and with the crowds around, probably drinking, it's the perfect time to make a move."

Hmm. I agree in principle, but from everything I've seen from the resistance so far, I'm not convinced they can pull it off. No, not they anymore. We. I'm all in with them.

"Do you really think people will be celebrating the parade after the stunt she just pulled?" I ask, hating even the hint of the memory of the executions.

"She executes people every day. This one was no different."

That's where I've gone wrong. To me, the execution is a big deal, because it's led to one of the biggest decisions in my entire life. But for people like Heather, who have already come to that realisation in the past, it's simply another day of horrors.

"What's the plan?" I ask.

"Oh no, I'm not telling you the plan." She laughs as if questioning my very sanity about the matter.

I purse my lips. I thought I'd managed to prove myself more than this by now. Apparently not.

"It's nothing personal, Chloe."

Not this time, anyway. She doesn't need to say it for me to know. She took an instant dislike to me, and things haven't improved since. Though I suppose she at least now tolerates my presence, which is better than nothing.

"I'm not telling anyone about the entire plan," she continues. "If you agree to take part in it, you'll be informed of *your* part, and yours only. That will be the case for every person taking part except for myself and a handful of others. That way, if anything goes wrong..."

"No one knows enough to get the rest of us into trouble and the resistance can continue," I finish for her.

It makes sense. I think I'd do the same in her position.

"Exactly. We must protect the majority. And some of the members have families who don't know about their role in the resistance. We need to keep their involvement as quiet as possible," she says.

I frown, resisting the urge to question why they wouldn't tell their families. It doesn't seem fair that innocent people may get caught up in this.

"People die," Heather says, clearly reading my thoughts from my face. "Especially here. Sometimes, people choose to try and make that stop rather than living in complacency."

Who am I to argue at that? I don't know what I'd choose if I had a family, I shouldn't be judging people in that situation.

"But that's neither here nor there. What I need to know is whether or not I can count on you to take part in the assassination?" Heather asks, her gaze boring into me.

I squirm a little, but think I manage to hold my own against her stern glare. She's not going to intimidate me into a life changing decision. Especially not one with so much risk attached to it.

But I can see why this is the resistance's only choice. In most places like this, getting rid of the Mayor won't work. But this entire city is her idea, and I refuse to believe there's anyone nearly as bad who could take over.

"Can I think about it?" I ask before I can blurt out a yes and seal my fate. No matter how I feel about the city and its need to fall, I have to think this through properly. It's probably time to get a message to Dimitri about what's going on too. I still haven't told them about the resistance, mostly because of Catherine's warnings. That, and I don't want them to tell me I have to stop.

"Yes. But don't take too long." It's impossible to tell from her expression if she's annoyed by my answer or not.

"Thank you."

I don't wait for her dismissal and get to my feet. Disappearing into the main room of the headquarters. She's given me a lot to think about, but I have to get out of there before I make a snap decision that will lead to my death.

CHAPTER SEVENTEEN

A KNOCK SOUNDS at my door, and I frown, confused by who it might be. I don't get much post, and it's still before the dusk siren, which makes the pool of who smaller. I don't think the sound is frantic enough for it to be anyone in trouble either.

I pad down the hall, glad I'm already dressed, even it's only in an oversized t-shirt and leggings, both of which are among the few items I brought with me from outside the wall.

I go up on my toes so I can look through the peephole. It's a little too high up the door for me, probably because the other agents have all been bigger men, and this apartment was set up for one of them. Though I can hardly imagine any of the agents I met while training living here, there isn't enough space for them.

The moment I spy Oscar's form on the other side of the door, I'm scrabbling to unlock it and let him in. There's no point asking how he got my address, we both know the answer to that one. Actually, that's not true. I don't know how he found it out, but I do know *when*.

"I brought breakfast," he announces the moment the door is open.

I chuckle. "What if I already ate?"

"Then there's more for me," he answers cheerfully. "Have you?"

"No. I was just making coffee." I step back so he can come into the apartment. There's nothing in here he can't see. To all intents and purposes, my life on the surface looks completely innocent.

"I didn't get any of that. I didn't know what you liked to drink when you wake up," he says as he follows me into the kitchen.

"Coffee and blood, normally." It's only when the words are out of my mouth that I remember I'm talking to someone human and not another vampire. I'm used to spending my time around the latter, especially in private.

He wrinkles his nose. "Together?"

"No, not together." I gesture to the two mugs sitting on the side. "Though some people specialise in those kinds of coffee," I admit.

"It doesn't sound great."

I chuckle. "Some vampires love it. I've never developed much of a taste for mixing my drinks like that."

"I don't think I would either. Coffee should just be coffee, nothing added."

"So I take it you want a black coffee with no sugar?" I ask as I open a cupboard and pull out one of my spare mugs. *Not* the ones I use for blood.

"If you don't mind." He sets the package of breakfast on the side. "Do you have plates?"

I set the mug up in the coffee machine and hit the on button. It whirs into motion.

"In the cupboard behind you," I direct.

He turns and pulls out two of the plates, then sets them down and begins unpacking what he's brought. I lick my lips as the smells are unleashed into the room. Whatever it is, it's better than anything I'd have made myself.

"Breakfast bagels," he answers my unspoken question. "They're one of my favourites."

"Where did you get them from? They smell delicious."

"I made them," he mumbles, almost too quietly for me to hear.

My heart skips a beat. He's made me breakfast and brought it all the way across the city. Though now I think about it, I have no idea where he lives. He could be my next-door neighbour for all I know. It's not something I'm going to ask, though. We already have somewhere we can spend time just the two of us. And the more I know, the more I can reveal if I'm ever captured.

The coffee machine beeps, and I grab his mug from underneath it, setting it down on the one tray I own alongside my two mugs. Horror rushes through me at the idea of drinking blood in front of him. What if that kind of thing freaks him out?

"Do you mind if I drink this?" I ask, my fingers still resting on the handle of my blood mug.

Oscar's eyebrows knit together. "Why would I mind?"

I shrug. "I'm sure some humans have a problem with this part of vampirism."

"I think they have more of a problem with the violence and death," he quips.

"Trust me, some vampires have a problem with that too," I admit, picking up the tray so I can take it into the small living room.

"I know they do," he assures me.

Oscar follows me into the living room and takes a seat next to me on the sofa. I place the tray on the small side table, and then take my plate from him.

"It looks delicious. Thank you." He has no idea

how much something like this means to me. I don't think I've ever had someone make me breakfast like this.

"You're welcome. I started to cook this evening and hated the idea of eating alone again. It wasn't until I was stood outside your door I even realised I was coming here," he admits sheepishly.

"I'm glad you came." My words are barely a whisper, but that doesn't make them any less true. It's lonely here, and I appreciate the company. Plus, the bagels really do look delicious.

I take a bite and close my eyes, enjoying the way the cheese, bacon, and hash browns taste together in the bagel.

"Is it okay?" he asks, his eyes full of nerves.

"It's delicious," I assure him once I've swallowed my mouthful. "You'll have to make these for me again."

A wide smile lights up his face, and I can understand why. I've basically just admitted I want to spend more alone time with him. If he'd done the same, then I'd be lighting up too.

"I can make them as often as you like."

"Thank you."

We eat the rest of our breakfast in silence, mostly because it's too delicious for me to be able to focus on anything other than the taste.

"Did you come here to help make up my mind about Heather's latest mission?" I ask him once I'm finished.

"No," he answers quickly. "I haven't even made up my mind, I wouldn't want to influence yours. It's going to be dangerous, and..." he trails off, as if thinking he's revealed too much.

"And?" I prompt.

He sighs and leans back in the sofa. "And I don't like the idea of you doing anything like that," he admits. "But before you say anything, I know that isn't my choice to make. And it's hypocritical of me to not want you in danger when everyone else would be. It just feels like so long since I had a..." he pauses, as if trying to find the right word.

What do I even want him to say? I'm not sure I have the answer to that.

"...friend," he finishes quietly, clearly unsure if that's what he wants to use.

I reach out and place a hand on his arm. "I understand. I haven't had anything like this in a long time either." In fact, I'm not sure if I've *ever* had anything like what Oscar and I are sharing.

Whatever it is, it's becoming clear both of us know it's something. It's too easy to be around him for just friends, but I don't know if I can do more.

Especially not with someone who doesn't know the truth about me.

The urge to tell him overcomes me, but I push it away. This isn't the time or the place. He has enough to worry about with the upcoming assassination plot. I don't want to add to that burden. He may not have officially decided yet, but I know it's not much of a choice for him really. Just like it isn't for me either.

Which means I *can't* tell him the truth on the off chance he gets caught. Or we'll end up like the people executed the other day. Heartbroken and forced to watch one another die.

CHAPTER EIGHTEEN

I CLEAR up the pots from the day before. Normally I do it after each meal, but Oscar has been spending more time here over the past few days, and I want to make the most of it. Which involves putting things off until he's gone.

My phone dings as I'm putting the dry plates away, and I wipe my hands off before grabbing it, expecting a text from him. When I unlock it, I don't find any notifications, which is when I realise it must have been my *other* phone.

Finally. Contact. It's been weeks, and I have no idea why.

I switch phones and pull up the messaging app we use. It's an encrypted one which will destroy messages ten minutes after they're read. I doubt it's fool proof, and most tech experts will be able to decode it within seconds, but it's better than nothing.

I grab a piece of paper so I can scribble down the message and make sure I get all of it before the screen goes blank. Ten minutes feels like a long time until you're trying to break a code. Then it's nothing more than a heartbeat. With it written down, I can take my time decoding and ensure everything is correct before burning all traces of it away.

Unsurprisingly, they want an update of how things are going. But that isn't the majority of the message. They've analysed everything that's been sent regarding the upcoming parade and they want me to find out more information about it. That stands to reason. It's something I've been trying to uncover more of too. I suspect it'll go easier if I agree to help with the plot to assassinate the Mayor. No doubt the resistance knows more than it's letting on about the parade itself.

Guilt surges through me at the idea of using the resistance to feed information to the vampires outside. I push it away. The two sides are working towards the same goal, what's the harm in them sharing intelligence? If I learn something new from the outside, then I can find a way to tell the resistance about it.

I turn on the hob and wait for the gas to light up

before holding the piece of paper over the open flames. Perhaps this isn't the best way to get rid of things, especially not when it risks setting off the fire alarm, but I need to make sure it's properly gone more than I need to avoid the annoying ringing.

The page curls up and turns into ash, dropping down onto the stove. Oops. I should have used a plate to burn it on. I keep making the same mistake while burning things. I'll try and do better next time.

With that done, I turn off the hob and return to the living room so I can sit comfortably while writing out my report for Bram and Dimitri. It won't be a very long one. Even with the resistance's help, I don't feel like I've learned very much of interest in the past couple of weeks.

Unless I count joining the resistance itself, but I'm hesitant to tell them about that as I don't want them to tell me to stop. Not only would that mean less time with Oscar, but also less chances for me to make a real difference to this city. And I don't want either of those.

I omit any mention of them from the report but do say I have a way of finding out more about the parade, and I hope to have more information on that soon. Hopefully, that's the perfect balance between the two things, while keeping all of my loyalties intact.

With that done, I switch phones again and pull up Heather's number. I'm only supposed to use it in emergencies, but I don't think she'll mind this time. I hit send before I can change my mind, and then stare at the words on the screen.

I'm in.

CHAPTER NINETEEN

THE RESISTANCE HEADQUARTERS is full of nervous excitement, which doesn't surprise me. Today is the day we've been waiting for, even though we haven't had long to prepare. Nerves flutter within me, but they're easy enough to ignore.

"All right, everyone, quiet down," Heather calls out.

Silence falls over the room as we all turn our attention to her. Not only is she in charge of the resistance, but this mission too. Listening to her will mean the difference between life and death. Though I do worry about us all being in the same room as one another. It means we can be used to identify other members of the resistance if the authorities manage to get hold of us. Then again, I can't tell them anything about anyone in the room other than a handful of forenames and maybe some descriptions. But appearances can be changed easily enough if there's no name to attach to them. I wish I bought some bleach to use on my hair if this all does go wrong.

Oscar slips his hand into mine and gives it a gentle squeeze.

"It'll be okay," he assures me softly.

I glance at him, noting the serious expression on his face. When he looks like this, he almost appears like his real age of twenty-six. I much prefer his boyish smiles. They make me feel young and carefree. A real feat when most humans would consider twenty-seven young, and vampires see it as barely more than a baby.

"As you all know, the parade is due to start in a few hours," Heather says, drawing my attention back to her. "We now know the route it's going to take, so please familiarise yourselves with that layout. For some of you, it may mean you have to adjust your instructions."

I need to check the map. I don't think Heather completely trusts me, as all she's done is given me a position as a lookout, which hasn't given me access to very much information to pass on to Bram and Dimitri. They're going to have to wait for my report after the fact to find out what's happening.

"No matter what happens, you need to hold your positions. If you see something happening to one of the other members of the team, then remember it could be part of the plan, and if you interfere, then you could end up destroying part of a carefully constructed plan," she instructs.

I frown. Something about her statement doesn't sit right. Is she expecting someone to get hurt from this? It doesn't seem likely that we can pull off this kind of thing without at least one person getting injured. Most likely the one pulling the trigger. But expecting us not to help one another if we're clearly in trouble is a step too far.

I'll make my decision on helping based on what I see in front of me. If it clearly isn't part of the plan, and I won't endanger anything else by stepping in, then I'll still do it. I don't want anyone to die if I can stop it from happening.

"We're doing a good thing, here," Heather shouts into the room.

People start to shuffle around more, and the atmosphere in the room flips into one of anticipation. Sometimes it's hard to remember everyone is here because they believe the City Of Blood needs to fall. I'm sure each person has their individual reasons, but they all amount to the same thing.

Which is why this plan may stand a chance at working.

"Today will go down in history as the day people in this city took a stance against the elite controlling it. None of them respect life, human or vampire. And now, we're going to teach them a lesson they won't forget." Heather is aflame with passion, but I'm not sure it's a good thing.

I hope she isn't going to try and seize power once the Mayor is gone. While she seems like a good choice to lead the resistance, I don't think she's a good choice for a free city. Especially not when she's so callously able to play with life.

In some ways, she isn't any better than the Mayor. In others, there's no competition. Heather doesn't condone cage fights, executions, or anything like that. Which is a step up after all.

Oscar squeezes my hand again. My shoulders relax, letting out some of the tension I wasn't aware they're holding. I don't think I'll be completely at ease until the dawn siren rings out across the city, letting me know the day is over. Though that won't mean we're safe. There's a lot more involved in getting away with this than simply assassinating the Mayor.

"Free the City Of Blood!" Heather cries.

"Free the City Of Blood!" everyone shouts back.

I exchange a look with Oscar, who seems as taken aback as I am by the sudden war cry. Perhaps he hasn't been involved in the resistance for as long as I think. There are some things we don't seem to talk about, and that's one of them. As is what he does during the day.

The crowd starts to disperse, going to check on the route and the other details of their role in the plan.

"Are you ready for this?" Oscar asks quietly.

I shake my head. "But that doesn't mean it isn't the right thing to do."

"It doesn't mean it is, either," he responds darkly.

I cock my head to the side. Is he having second thoughts about being a part of this? Should I say something to give him hope?

Oscar laughs lightly, completely blowing away his previous mood. "I'm sorry, ignore me. I'm nervous."

"That's no reason to ignore you," I assure him. "The opposite."

He smiles reassuringly. "I need to go check my part of the route," he says.

"Me too." Especially as I have no doubt my position will have changed so I can see more of what's going on.

"Are you going to tell me where you're stationed so we can meet up after?" he asks.

"No." Saying the word to him pains me, but I know I must. "But we can agree to meet at my apartment after? We can spend all day together, if you don't have anything else on."

He nods. "I'd like that. Thank you."

He leans in and kisses my cheek, before finally letting go of my hand and walking off towards one of the map stations.

I raise my hand to my cheek and press my fingers against the spot he kissed. The skin still tingles, though perhaps it's in my imagination.

I stand there for a moment, trying to build up the courage to go look at one of the maps myself. Whether I want to admit it or not, I'm scared. For some reason, I have an ominous feeling about what's coming. I hope it's just nerves and squish it down. This is the right thing to do. The Mayor's reign needs to be over, and we're going to make it happen.

CHAPTER TWENTY

I MUST ADMIT, the position Heather has picked out for me has a great view of the main square and most of the parade route. I hope it means I can make a difference if something goes wrong. Though I'm not completely sure about how I'm supposed to communicate with anyone, especially if we're not supposed to interfere if something goes wrong.

I pace back and forth while I wait, trying to ignore the festive atmosphere and how wrong it feels. It shouldn't surprise me that people find amusement in the antics of the city. Some of the vampires love the cage fights, and I suspect they're some of the ones here. On the human front, I'm not sure what the appeal is, but I can smell a lot of them in the crowd.

Not for the first time, and probably not the last

either, I pluck at my armband, checking it's in place. Every member of the resistance involved in the plan is wearing them, to make them easy to identify for the lookouts like me. But I'm not sure they're a good idea. If one of the guards works out what they mean, then all of us will end up on the execution stand by the end of the day.

My gaze slips to the scaffold in the centre of the square. I haven't been here often enough to know if it's there all the time, or if it's been put up so it can be used today. I'm sure it'll see action before the end of the day. From everything I've heard about the other anniversary events, it's likely the streets will run red with blood by dawn.

I tear my eyes away and search for the resistance member closest to me. My focus catches on to the middle-aged woman in question. I don't know her name, but I've seen her around headquarters several times. I wonder if she's one of the people with families who don't know about her involvement in this. I hope Heather hasn't let anyone like that take part in today's mission, but I'm not convinced she'll have thought about that. Or cares about it all. She's the kind of woman who only focuses on the results.

Satisfied the woman is in position and not in any danger, I start searching the surrounding area, trying to work out if any of the people around her may pose a threat. There's still fifteen minutes or so until the parade is due to pass through, which gives me just enough time to do some proper checks. At least, I hope so.

A resistance armband catches my attention. There shouldn't be anyone else in the vicinity, so who is this?

The man gestures around and points to his armband, then says something else. Which is when it finally hits me who he's talking to.

Guards.

I scan back a little further and notice more heavily armoured guards further back.

Dread floods through me.

We've been betrayed.

I rip my armband off and stuff it in my pocket, not wanting to draw extra attention to myself if I can help it. Especially if the guards now know how to identify us.

I scan the square, trying to find where Heather is. She's the only person who knows where everyone is, and that means she can get us all out. If I pass anyone else with a resistance band, then I can tell them to take it off too.

Eventually, I spot her, and don't waste any time making my way towards her. My pulse pounds in my ears, so much it drowns out the sounds of everyone else's around me, and with the number of humans around, that's impressive to say the least.

The crowd jostles against me, and I almost get lost a couple of times, but manage to right my course. I just hope Heather hasn't moved between me spotting her and getting to the right place.

"Excuse me please," I mutter as I push through people, hating that I'm having to do it. I can't stand being rude to people, especially strangers who have done nothing wrong in the first place. "Can I squeeze through, please?"

No one answers me. They're too busy taking advantage of the cheap food and drink from stalls around the square.

I breathe a sigh of relief when I push through one last set of people and almost run straight into Heather.

Her eyes lock onto mine, and anger flares up within them.

"We've been compromised," I blurt out before she can even start scolding me. I don't care how unhappy she is with me for leaving my post, there are lives at stake and that's all I'm interested in.

"Because you're out of your position. Get back to it," she says firmly.

"The guards know that the bands mean someone is part of the resistance," I tell her. "At the very least we can tell people to take their bands off. It's a safety..."

"Get back into your position, Chloe, and stop wasting my time." Heather's expression is hard, and I doubt there's any changing her mind.

If we all get through this alive, which I'm starting to doubt, then she's going to kick me out of the resistance for certain. At this point, I'm not sure I care. I don't want to be part of anything that puts so little value on life.

"We have to stop this. They're going to catch us and kill us all," I insist.

"This is none of your concern." Heather pushes me to the side as she speaks. "Get back to your post or leave completely. But if you get in my way again, then I *will* kill you."

The expression on her face is enough to convince me she's telling the truth, and that I never plan on following her in anything ever again.

I watch her leave, running through my options of what to do now. I could go back to my post like she wants me to. Or I could run around and find everyone with an armband and tell them to take it off, but I doubt that'll work. Some people will still go through with part of the plan. Others won't believe me, and I won't find others.

But I need to save them.

And Oscar.

My eyes widen. He'll believe me. And he's been part of the resistance for longer than I have. No doubt that means some of the others will believe him faster than they would me. He may even know some of their phone numbers. And it has the added benefit of me being certain he's safe.

The only problem is that I have no idea what part of the square he's in, or how to get there. I'm going to have to look for him the hard way. At least that means I can try and save some of the resistance members if I pass them too. I just hope they'll listen.

CHAPTER TWENTY-ONE

"You need to take your armband off, the guards know how to recognise us," I tell a woman.

She raises an eyebrow but doesn't say anything.

"Please. And tell the others," I beg her.

I've lost count of how many members of the resistance I've told the same thing, I just hope some of them have taken my warning seriously.

"I recognise you," she says, finally breaking the odd silence. "You're Oscar's stakeout partner."

I nod enthusiastically. "I'm looking for him now, do you know where he is?"

She studies me for a moment, trying to decide whether it's safe to tell me. I don't blame her, and I'm grateful someone so diligent is near him in the square. It means he's been safe from harm this whole time.

"He's over by the foot of the scaffold," she says. "I'm not sure what he's supposed to be doing there."

"Me neither," I answer honestly, both hopeful and horrified now I've learned where he is. "Please consider taking the band off, it isn't safe."

She nods and tears it away. Relief floods through me as a result. At least she's one person I may be able to save.

"Have you told Heather about this?" the woman asks.

"Yes, but she refused to believe me." Which is only the half of it, really. I believed her when she said she'd kill me.

"That sounds about right. She's a stubborn one. And that isn't always a good thing," the woman says. "Good luck finding your man."

I'm about to respond that Oscar isn't my man, but it doesn't matter what she thinks, and its precious time I can be using to get to him. I still have a large part of the square to cross before I'm even in the vicinity of the construction, and even then, I'll have to go around it to find his exact location.

I wave at her in a vague goodbye, and start heading over to where the imposing structure looms over us all. I dodge between both humans and vampires, trying not to get in anyone's way.

It only takes a couple of minutes to get there, but

it feels like it's taken an age. A man with a resistance armband stands with his back to me, and I sigh with relief that I'm not going to have to waste precious time looking for him.

"Oscar!" I call when I'm close enough for him to hear.

He spins around, and his face lights up as he sees me, only to then furrow with concern.

I rush up to him and launch myself into his arms. He hugs me tightly but is tense beneath my grasp.

"What's wrong, Chloe?" he asks once I pull back.

"Take your armband off." I reach off and tug on it until it comes free, not wanting to wait any longer than I have to. "We've been betrayed. Heather threatened to kill me when I told her. But they're going to start rounding up resistance members soon. We need to get out of here. And warn anyone we can," I babble.

"Wait, slow down. Go again. How do you know we've been betrayed?" he asks.

"I saw one of our members instructing the guards on how to tell which of us are members."

He nods. "I have a few of their numbers. Let me send a message and then we should get out of here."

I sigh with relief, grateful he hasn't taken any convincing on the matter. The last thing I want is for Oscar not to believe or trust me.

He pulls out his phone and fires off the message. "Hopefully, that will do the trick. I doubt all of them will listen, but so long as some of them do, we can call this a win."

I nod. "I felt the same when talking to the people I ran into while trying to find you."

He slips his hand into mine and gives it a squeeze. I can get used to this form of reassurance, it's more powerful than any words he could say.

We start to make our way out of the square, pushing back through the people I've just cut through, though I doubt any of them thinking twice about it.

A loud rhythmic thumping fills the air, stopping us in our tracks as we realise our way out is blocked. The parade is here, whether we like it or not.

Which means the assassination attempt is about to happen if we haven't managed to reach enough of the resistance in time.

I shrink back into Oscar, who puts his arms around me and holds me tight as the parade starts to go past.

At first, there's nothing particularly special about it, other than guards walking in formation, some of them with drums, and others with trumpets, announcing the arrival of the rest.

Some acrobats come next, jumping, and twirling

as they go past. It's almost joyful, as if there's nothing wrong with the world we live in. The crowd cheers as one of the tumblers does a particularly impressive trick.

"Why is this making me feel worse instead of better?" I mutter under my breath.

"Because this is the mask an abuser wears," Oscar responds darkly.

I hope no one is listening to us, or we could get into a lot of trouble for our comments. I doubt people are paying attention to us, though. Not when there's so much going on in front of us.

Bile rises in my throat as the next float comes past. A large metal cage sits at the centre of it, with two scared people within it.

"Fight! Fight! Fight!" People in the crowd cry as the float passes, the flood lights which light the entire square are only enhancing the horror of the cage. Especially as there is another, smaller, one on the float with a dozen people crammed inside it.

No doubt they're the other victims who will be shoved into the main cage every time someone dies.

A tear rolls down my cheeks and splashes against Oscar's hand. He tightens his hold around me. I'm not sure how I would be dealing with this if he wasn't with me.

The cage fight float passes, making way for one

with what appears to be burlesque dancers. I'm not sure where the Mayor has found them from, but they titillate the crowd with a series of raunchy dances, complete with flourishes of feathers, and swaying hips.

A woman behind us gasps loudly. "How inappropriate. There are children here," she cries.

"Because the cage fights are child friendly," Oscar mutters under his breath.

I reach up and place a hand over his where it holds me and give it a squeeze. If he can do it to offer me comfort, then I can do the same back to him.

My attention pulls away from the dancers and towards the float a few down. It's the biggest by far and includes a colossal throne. Even if I didn't already know what the Mayor looks like, I'd have been able to guess that's who the woman perched on the throne is.

"Do you think they're still going to try the plan?" I ask.

"Probably," he admits. "Heather isn't the kind of woman who lets her plans fail."

"That's what I'm afraid of," I agree, keeping my eyes trained on the float. I don't know anything about what they have planned, which makes it hard to watch for the warning signs, whatever they're going to be.

A shot fires over the crowd, making me flinch.

"They have guns?" I whisper.

Oscar shrugs. "I have no idea. None that I've ever seen, but that doesn't mean anything."

We try to move away, but the crowd starts to panic as more shots ring out and they realise something potentially deadly is happening. My pulse is frantic along with them, and the adrenaline brings out my fangs.

That's bad news. It means other vampires are likely to be having the same response. And if they're hungry too...

A shiver runs down my spine at the thought of the disaster which could be about to unfold in front of us.

Several people with resistance armbands break through the crowd and begin to try and storm the float. I don't recognise any of them other than Heather. I hope none of them are the ones I warned. When this goes south, Heather will no doubt blame me for scaremongering, when really, I've been trying to save lives.

Another shot rings out, but it's too late. The Mayor is already gone. She's hiding inside her float, which is no doubt bulletproof.

Guards rush into the crowd, using their own guns, as well as their fangs to try and calm people down.

I pull away from Oscar, but still hold onto his hand. The last thing I want is to lose him in the riled-up crowd.

The scent of fresh blood hits my nose, and panic begins to set in. I've been trained to resist some of my baser urges, but I'm not immune to spilled blood. And neither are the poorer vampires in the city who may not have had blood for days. They're going to turn the humans apart.

And I don't know what to do about it.

Some of the guards rush in and start separating people into which of the two species they are. If I'm not careful, I'm going to end up on the opposite side of the divide from Oscar, and I don't rate my chances of getting out of here if that happens.

"We need to go," I say, tugging on his sleeve.

He nods, and we start pushing through the crowd. I keep my eyes peeled for anyone bleeding, both so I can prepare myself for the scent, and also to check no one is attacking them. While we have to get out of here, I won't do it at the detriment of any kind of life.

A blur comes from my left and I spin around in time to see a feral looking vampire with his fangs bared flying at a little girl. I'm about to jump in when Oscar moves first. He throws himself into the path of the vampire, sending the two of them tumbling.

I start to move forward to help Oscar but remember the little girl. I need to watch her and check no other desperate vampires try to drink from her. I'm not sure where her guardians are, but I hope they turn up soon. Being a vampire myself, I don't think the best thing for me to do is start talking to the terrified youngster.

A scream rips from my throat, but it's lost among the rest of the noise in the square.

The two men grapple for dominance as they roll around on shards of broken glass. Small flashes of glass came from their clothes and hair.

One of the little girl's parents appears and scoops her off, giving me one less thing to focus on. But the distraction costs me, as when I turn back to Oscar, the vampire is pulling a long shard of glass from his stomach.

Pain lances through me at the sight. What has he done?

A guard rushes over and pulls the vampire away, locking him in handcuffs and dragging him away. I'm about to ask him what he's going to do to help Oscar, but he doesn't come back.

I rush over to my friend's side and drop to my

knees, picking up his hand in mine and giving it a squeeze.

"Can you walk if I help you?" I ask him. We're not far from the Black Fan. If I can get him there, maybe Catherine will be able to help.

He nods weakly, his skin deathly pale. But I have to try. I *can't* watch him die. I pull off my jacket and ball it up so I can stick it under his t-shirt and hopefully stem the flow of blood.

Carefully, I pull him to his feet and drape his arm around mine. Slowly, we start to make our way down the street. I hope anyone watching will dismiss us as drunks, and not as a mortally wounded human escorted by a vampire. That will lead to questions I don't want to answer.

I pause as a group of guards run past, dragging a bound member of the resistance behind them. They throw her in with a group of the others. Heather is clinging to the bars with fire in her expression. I meet her gaze, and she narrows her eyes, and it becomes clear in my mind that she's going to blame me for everything that went wrong today.

I'm not completely sure she's wrong, but I can't devote any of my attention to that. I must get Oscar to safety before he bleeds out.

CHAPTER TWENTY-TWO

We burst through the door just in time, as Oscar collapses onto the floor of the brothel.

"I'll go get Lady Catherine," Sonia says after taking one look at me. She rushes out of the room. I hope she isn't about to report us.

I start trying to make Oscar comfortable, but fear I'm failing miserably. He's losing too much blood, and it's making it impossible to make him comfortable.

"Chloe, what happened?" Catherine asks as she rushes into the room. It's taken her less time than I expected to get here. Perhaps she was only in the other room.

"He's been stabbed." I lift the bottom of Oscar's shirt to reveal the gash there.

Catherine's nose wrinkles, but she doesn't give

any other sign that she's affected by the blood. Perhaps it's an age thing. I'll ask later, if I can remember.

"Benedict," she says, summoning her companion.

"Oh, I'm sorry, I didn't realise you were with a client." I bow my head, only now realising how much danger I've put everyone in.

Catherine gives a small snort. "Benedict's my husband, not a client. Luckily for you, we're closed tonight."

I breathe a sigh of relief as her words sink in.

She turns to the man again. "Can you take the young man and Chloe up to the spare room? I'll get the things she needs to tend to his wound."

Benedict nods and moves forward to scoop up Oscar as if he's a child.

"Thank you," I say to Catherine.

She shakes her head. "Save your thanks until after we've saved him. Anything before then is a waste of breath."

My eyes widen, and the horror of what's about to happen sinks in. We have to act quickly now we're here.

"Go with Benedict," she instructs. "He'll get you settled."

I nod and hurry after the other vampire, feeling safe for the first time today, and knowing I'm lucky

Catherine hasn't decided to turn us away. If we were on the streets, then Oscar wouldn't stand a chance.

* * *

"He isn't going to make it," Catherine says, handing me a clean cloth to use on Oscar.

"You don't know that." The desperation in my voice is impossible to miss, and even I know the reason I'm saying it is because I don't *want* to lose Oscar. He's become too important in my life, even in a short amount of time.

"I do. I've seen humans at this stage of death more times than I care to count. The only option you have now is to turn him," the courtesan says as she takes a seat at the end of the bed.

A tear rolls down my cheek and splashes onto the covers next to Oscar. For the first time in my life, I find myself wishing I was something other than a vampire so I can make a difference to him.

"Turning him is illegal," I say weakly.

"It is."

"Wouldn't that be the wrong thing to do?" I ask.

"I suppose it depends what you think he wants," Catherine responds. "I don't have the answer for you. He's your friend, which means you're the one with the best chance of making the right decision."

"I don't want him to die," I whisper.

"What you want, and what's right, are often two different things."

I wish she'd stop being so wise and reasonable all the time.

Oscar lets out a low moan, and I glance down at his clammy face, my heart breaking at the sight. I reach out and brush a strand of dark hair away from his forehead.

"He wants to make a difference in the world," I whisper. "I don't think he's done yet."

I turn my attention to Catherine to find the woman smiling, like she knew what I was going to say the entire time.

"Then you know what to do." She rises to her feet and heads for the door. "You can call me when it's done. The two of you are welcome to stay here until the turning is complete, but I won't be able to hide you after that. Too many important people come through here."

"Thank you," I whisper.

"You're welcome. Your friend isn't the only one in this room who wants to help people." With that, she leaves the room, letting the door click shut behind her.

I look down at Oscar again, preparing myself for what I know I must do. I've never turned someone before, but I know how it works. The only problem is that it may cause us problems after, especially with the resistance leadership now in custody. No one will know how to get us out of the city.

But if I don't act soon, there won't be an us to make the decision at all.

I'm already condemned multiple times over. What's the harm in breaking the law one more time? I close my eyes and prepare myself to bite. No matter what happens next, there's no going back.

Thank you for reading *Drop Of Blood*, I hope you enjoyed it. Chloe's story continues in *Drought Of Blood*: http://books2read.com/droughtofblood

You can also download a prologue of Chloe arriving in the City Of Blood here: https://dl.bookfunnel.com/5zjkrhhols

AUTHOR NOTE

Thank you for taking the time to read Drop Of Blood. I hope you enjoyed it! Chloe and Oscar will be back in book 2, Drought Of Blood, where they'll have to deal with the consequences of their actions! If you've read some of my other books set in The Obscure World, then you may have noticed some returning characters - Bram from the Ashryn Barker Trilogy, and Catherine from Bite Of The Past. There was also a very brief mention of Grimalkin Academy, where vampires and witches go to a university level academy together. I have several series set there! If you haven't read either of those, then don't worry, you won't need to in order to continue the story, I try and write all of my series as entry points into the world. If you read them all, you'll simply

AUTHOR NOTE

have seen a bigger picture of what the Obscure World is.

There's also a prequel to the City Of Blood series - Blood Payment, which follows Reese as she set up the City Of Blood thirty years ago. While I haven't included exact dates in the series (I don't like doing that as it often dates it!), I can tell you informally that the City Of Blood was founded in 1990 (though in hindsight, I should perhaps have picked a date that wasn't before I was born!)

I hope you continue the journey into the City Of Blood with me. I've had so much fun with both the characters and the setting...as well as creeping myself out at some points!

A note on Chapter 13: The books mentioned during Chloe and Oscar's discussion are real and are my (current) favourites from two of my best friends and co-authors. The cat assassins belong to the Catnip Assassins series by Skye MacKinnon (starts with Meow), and the detective with a hellhound puppy belongs to the Samantha Rain Mysteries by Arizona Tape (starts with The Case Of The Night Mark). I love both and would recommend them to anyone who loves strong heroines, animals, and urban fantasy! (They also don't know I've done this...so Skye, Ari, if you're reading, your books are awesome!)

Happy Reading!
Laura

ALSO BY LAURA GREENWOOD

Books in the Paranormal Council Universe

- The Paranormal Council Series (shifter romance, completed series)
- The Fae Queen Of Winter Trilogy (paranormal/fantasy)
- Spring Fae Duology (paranormal/fantasy)
- Thornheart Coven Series (witch romance)
- Return Of The Fae Series (paranormal post-apocalyptic, completed series)
- Paranormal Criminal Investigations Series (urban fantasy mystery)
- MatchMater Paranormal Dating App Series (paranormal romance, completed series)
- The Necromancer Council Trilogy (urban fantasy)
- Standalone Stories From the Paranormal Council Universe

Books in the Obscure World

- Ashryn Barker Trilogy (urban fantasy,

completed series)
- Grimalkin Academy: Kittens Series (paranormal academy, completed series)
- Grimalkin Academy: Catacombs Trilogy (paranormal academy, completed series)
- City Of Blood Trilogy (urban fantasy)
- Grimalkin Academy: Stakes Trilogy (paranormal academy)
- The Harpy Bounty Hunter Trilogy (urban fantasy)
- Bite Of The Past (paranormal romance)
- Sabre Woods Academy (paranormal academy)
- The Shadow Seer Association (urban fantasy)

Books in the Forgotten Gods World

- The Queen of Gods Trilogy (paranormal/mythology romance)
- Forgotten Gods Series (paranormal/mythology romance, completed series)

The Grimm World

- Grimm Academy Series (fairy tale

academy)
- Fate Of The Crown Duology (Arthurian Academy)
- Once Upon An Academy Series (Fairy Tale Academy)

Other Series

- Untold Tales Series (urban fantasy fairy tales)
- The Dragon Duels Trilogy (urban fantasy dystopia)
- ME Contemporary Standalones (contemporary romance)
- Standalones
- Seven Wardens, co-written with Skye MacKinnon (paranormal/fantasy romance, completed series)
- The Firehouse Feline, co-written with Lacey Carter Andersen & L.A. Boruff (paranormal/urban fantasy romance)
- Kingdom Of Fairytales Snow White, co-written with J.A. Armitage (fantasy fairy tale)

Twin Souls Universe

- Twin Souls Trilogy, co-written with Arizona Tape (paranormal romance, completed series)
- Dragon Soul Series, co-written with Arizona Tape (paranormal romance, completed series)
- The Renegade Dragons Trilogy, co-written with Arizona Tape (paranormal romance, completed series)
- The Vampire Detective Trilogy, co-written with Arizona Tape (urban fantasy mystery, completed series)
- Amethyst's Wand Shop Mysteries Series, co-written with Arizona Tape (urban fantasy)

Mountain Shifters Universe

- Valentine Pride Trilogy, co-written with L.A. Boruff (paranormal shifter romance, completed series)
- Magic and Metaphysics Academy Trilogy, co-written with L.A. Boruff (paranormal academy, completed series)
- Mountain Shifters Standalones, co-written with L.A. Boruff (paranormal romance)

Audiobooks: www.authorlauragreenwood.co.uk/p/audio.html

ABOUT THE AUTHOR

Laura is a USA Today Bestselling Author of paranormal and fantasy romance. When she's not writing, she can be found drinking ridiculous amounts of tea, trying to resist French Macaroons, and watching the Pitch Perfect trilogy for the hundredth time (at least!)

FOLLOW THE AUTHOR

- Website: www.authorlauragreenwood.co.uk
- Mailing List: www.authorlauragreenwood.co.uk/p/mailing-list-sign-up.html
- Facebook Group: http://facebook.com/groups/theparanormalcouncil
- Facebook Page: http://facebook.com/authorlauragreenwood
- Bookbub: www.bookbub.com/authors/laura-greenwood

- Instagram: www.instagram.com/authorlauragreenwood
- Twitter: www.twitter.com/lauramg_tdir

Printed in Great Britain
by Amazon

44396873R00109